StringNet
教你使用英文同義字（III）

李路得●著

英語辭彙不NG

本書介紹

線上語料庫是甚麼？

　　英語線上語料庫（corpus）是新興的英語學習工具。傳統字典的例句及教科書的文章大多是為教學而刻意寫作，常被質疑和英美人士實際使用的英文不盡相同，英語線上語料庫則是蒐集真實語料如英美國家的報章雜誌，將其中的單字或片語加以整理彙編，透過網路提供使用者在線上搜尋某一個單字或片語出現的所有句子。目前世界各種語言有許多已經建立其語料庫，英語最大的語料庫則是BNC（British National Corpus）語料庫，內容涵蓋英美國家的報章雜誌、學術論文、小說、廣播節目等真實語料，蒐集單字量超過一億。英語學習者可以藉由語料庫查詢單字及片語上下文及其前後出現的搭配詞，以了解精準意義及用法，以此方式能夠學習真實世界的英語用法，特別在英文寫作的遣詞用字上有明顯裨益。

StringNet是甚麼？

　　在BNC語料庫（http://www.natcorp.ox.ac.uk/）中，英文單字與片語只有經過簡單初步的彙整，後來拜科技之賜，有一些學者把BNC的內容作進一步詳細的分類，能夠查詢更多資訊，本書採用的StringNet（http://www.lexchecker.org/index.php）是國立中央大學特聘研究講座David Wible教授主持創立的多功能英語線上語料庫查詢系統，內容以BNC（British National Corpus）語料庫為主，整理其中單字及片語，計算某個單字在語料庫出現的次數，若該單字有二種詞類，亦分別計算列出，以recruit為例，它可以當動詞和名詞，其動詞出現1934次，名詞出現871次；也分析某單字常常和那些搭配詞一起使用，提供片語字串，如recruit from和recruit new members等；還可依搭配詞的詞類分別檢索，並顯示搭配詞在語料庫中出現的次數從最多到最少，如recruit當動詞時後面出現的複數名詞有staff（28次）、

people（21次）、members（13次）、student（9次）、workers（6次）、women（6次）等等，其中staff出現最多次，由此可知這二個字時常一起使用；除了顯示和常用搭配詞形成的字串以外，StringNet也提供包含某單字或片語的所有完整句子。

如何使用本書？

由於StringNet的功能複雜，不易學習完整檢索方法，因此本書針對單字搭配詞的部分整理彙編，以俾讀者學習某一單字常用那些搭配詞，及這些搭配詞是否有共同特點（例如前面動詞recruit後面出現的受詞都是人類），並且把一組同義字合併彙整討論，以比較同義字之間的搭配詞有否差異。

本書的目的在於釐清意義容易混淆的英文單字，編排時以中文意義為考量，而非英文單字的拼法，因此本書內容是按照中文注音符號的順序排列，已經出版第一冊包含ㄅ到ㄈ，第二冊包含ㄉ到ㄍ，本書為第三冊，也是最後一冊，包含ㄎ到ㄩ。

本書包含90組同義字，每一組的內容分為四部份：

1.語料庫出現次數

藉著比較各同義字在語料庫出現的次數多寡顯示各單字的常用程度，例如：

StringNet語料庫出現次數

flatter	insinuate	fawn
482 (v.)	92 (v.)	42 (v.)

在此表示動詞flatter在StringNet中的出現次數是482次，動詞insinuate出現92次，動詞fawn出現42次。

2.常用句型和例句

　　幫助讀者明白每個單字可以出現的句子結構以及例句，建立上下語文情境的概念，例如不及物動詞（vi.）後面不能出現受詞，或某些動詞常用在被動語態，例如：

> **S + flatter + O（+ about/ on + N）**
> **S + be flattered + that 子句**
> **S + flatter oneself that 子句**

The employees were eager to **flatter** their boss at his birthday party.

His praise **flattered** her vanity, even though she didn't like him at all.

She **flattered herself that** she was the most attractive girl at the party.

3.常用搭配詞

　　若要探討的單字是及物動詞，則提供該動詞前面常用的主詞和後面常用的受詞；若是不及物動詞，則提供該前面常用的主詞和後面常用的介系詞或副詞；若是形容詞，則提供後面常用的名詞；但是不一定全部都提供，會斟酌個別單字的使用情形。以動詞swing為例，常用的主詞如下：

（det.）_n._ + swing

door, arms, legs, pendulum hair, mood, wind, opinion, men, foot, tail, sign, boy, fish, gates, boat, hand.

在此（det.）表示可能出現限定詞a、the，所有格或量詞等，_n._ 表示下方所列的單字可出現在此位置，下方名詞從door到hand是依照在語料庫出現次數從多到少依序排列，也就是說door最常用作swing的主詞。在StringNet有完整句子，例如The front door swung open and Mrs Vigo came in, holding the child.（http://www.lexchecker.org/hyngram/hyngram_ex.php?hyngram_cjson=[30,%20287969]&meta_offset=105834492）

swing常用的受詞如下:
swing +（det.）_n._
　　leg, axe, balance, door, club, pendulum gun, rod, bat, stick, gate, handle, scarf, hammer, basket, bag.

4.綜合整理

　　在此解釋同一組同義字個別單字的中文意義，參考Longman online Dictionary（http：//www.ldoceonline.com/）, the Free Dictionary by Farlex（http://www.thefreedictionary.com/）等線上字典，並說明搭配詞的特性，以幫助讀者比較同義字之間意義與搭配詞的異同，在寫作時能選擇正確的單字及正確的搭配詞。全書最後並有單字索引，可以依照字母順序查考單字。

目　次

Unit 1 渴望

StringNet語料庫出現次數

desire	lust	crave	covet
5638 (n.) 1408 (v.)	490 (n.) 33 (v.)	310 (v.)	51 (v.) 138 (coveted)

desire（n.）

❖ 例句

The visitors expressed a desire to see the farther end of the garden.
遊客們表示很想看一看這個花園更裡面的一端。
He had no desire to move anywhere.
他一點都不想搬家。

❖ 常用搭配詞

v. + a desire
express, have, reflect, indicate, feel, show, fight, create, declare.

Vpp + by the/a desire to do something
motivated, influenced, inspired, possessed, prompted, fired, driven, dominated,

a + _adj._ + desire to do something

strong, genuine, burning, real, great, positive, natural, sudden, wild, general, simple, powerful, desperate, terrible, keen, primitive, secret, compelling, slight, fierce, common, judicial.

desire for + _n._

peace, revenge, change, food, power, knowledge, profit, unity, vengeance, coffee, recognition, independence, freedom, marriage, pleasure, order, victory, truth, solitude, control, reform, comfort, money, secrecy.

desire（vt.）

❖ 常用句型

> **S + desire + to do something**
> **S + desire + that 子句**

❖ 例句

He desired to return to his homeland.
他渴望回去他的祖國。

The protector desires that, prior to his coronation, the king should not be seen too frequently in public.
保護者希望國王在加冕之前不要太常在出現在公共場合。

His job performance in the past year left much to be desired.
他過去一年的工作表現有待改進。

❖ 常用搭配詞

desired + n.

effect, result, behavior, level, track, record, end, direction, output, response, goal, object, height, shape, strength, position, ratio, way, performance, improvement, temperature, action, number, change, aim, situation, information, location, transformation, balance, accuracy.

desire + to v.

have, make, give, do, see, take, avoid, know, keep, live, speak, obtain, buy, leave, refer, show, hold, afford, reduce, move, resume, add, alter, go, retain, appropriate, close, emulate, win, bring, remain, meet.

lust（n.）

❖ 例句

The media have whetted a lust for sensationalism that has turned us into a nation of accident watchers.
媒體一昧地追求聳動的新聞，使得國人變得熱衷於意外事件的報導。

❖ 常用搭配詞

lust for + n.

life, power, glory, love, revenge.

adj. + lust

male, pure, teenage, sexual, physical, hot, mutual, mad.

lust（vi.）

❖ 常用句型

> **S + lust after/for somebody/something**

❖ 例句

He has silently lusted after a woman who is married to a merchant.
他一直暗戀一個商人的妻子。

❖ 常用搭配詞

adv. + lust
　just, violently, silently, still.

crave（vi./vt.）

❖ 常用句型

> **S + crave（for）+ O**

❖ 例句

Politicians crave for power as alcoholics crave for drink.
政客渴求權力如同酒精成癮者渴望喝酒。
He is controlling his diet and craving for fast-food.
他在節食並控制他對速食的慾望。

❖ 常用搭配詞

crave for + n.

  success, power, drink.

crave + n.

  food, success, affection.

coveted（adj.）

❖ 例句

He won the coveted job.
他得到這份人人欣羨的工作。

❖ 常用搭配詞

coveted + n.

  prize, trophy, job, gold, title, position, role, award, crown, fellowship, part,
  places, posts, contract.

covet（vt.）

❖ 常用句型

S + covet + O

❖ 例句

You shall not covet your neighbor's wife.
不可貪戀鄰舍的妻子。

❖ 常用搭配詞

covet one's + n.
　house, wife, object, position, practice.

綜合整理

desire	及物動詞，正式用字，表示渴望得到某個東西，受詞若是人，表示想和某人發生性關係。後面較常接不定詞（to do something）表示想做某事，或接that子句表示希望事情如何發展。常用在被動語態（如leave much to be desired）或過去分詞當形容詞。
lust	表示肉慾（lust after + 人）或貪戀自己不需要的東西（lust for + 事物），有負面意義。
crave	極強烈的渴望，比desire程度較強。後面有時接for，但是意義不變。
covet	正式用字。指貪戀別人的東西，時常用過去分詞coveted + N表示大家都覬覦的東西。另外covetous表示貪戀的（如covetous eyes/desires/rivals）。

Unit 2 開明的

StringNet語料庫出現次數

liberal	enlightened
5332	447

liberal（adj.）

❖ 例句

Holland's liberal attitude is held as a model by many pro-euthanasia campaigners.
荷蘭的開明態度被許多贊成安樂死的社會運動人士視為典範。

❖ 常用搭配詞

liberal + n.

view, interpretation, tradition, approach, society, principles, attitude, support, opinion, thought, politics, economics, policy, position.

enlightened（adj.）

❖ 例句

Which one is better, enlightened absolutism or democracy?
開明專制和民主哪一個比較好？
He took a more enlightened viewpoint of this matter.
他對這件事情抱持比較開明的觀點。

❖ 常用搭配詞

enlightened + n.

self-interest, despotism, attitude, view, despot, government, policy, ruler, approach, public, bureaucrats, self, members, times, amateurs, management, days, circles, employers, man, age, rule, opinion, treatment, teaching, firms, people, companies, reform, state, friend.

綜合整理

liberal	願意去了解及尊重他人的想法和感受。此字有多種意義，常出現在政治用語表示自由主義的。後面接的名詞多半不是人，少數是人的情況則是指美國民主黨員（如Liberal Democrat, Liberal leader）。
enlightened	對事情抱持明智的態度且對人則以公平仁慈對待。前面常接比較級more，後面的名詞可以是人或事物，常用在enlightened absolutism（開明專制）和enlightened self-interest（開明的自利）。

Unit 3 抗議，異議

StringNet語料庫出現次數

protest	objection	dissent
3894	2550	466

protest（n.）

❖ 例句

A boy has provoked a storm of protest after posting a video that shows him abusing a turtle.

一個男孩在網路上傳他虐待一隻烏龜的影片後引起輿論撻伐。

He resigned in protest at the government's new economic policy.

他辭職以表示對政府的新經濟政策的抗議。

❖ 常用搭配詞

v. + a protest

stage, sign, lodge, leading, register, hold, issue, address, make, attend, organize, call.

adj. + protest

public, political, violent, mass, strong, peaceful, anti-government, popular, further, widespread, formal, official, angry, social, diplomatic, working-class, effective, nationwide, anti-war, nationalist, continuing, moral, massive, fierce, renewed, large, growing, token, vehement, silent, student-led, personal, disorderly, initial, spontaneous, organized, outraged, radical, revolutionary, environmental.

protest + _n._

march, movement, vote, group, action, strike, demonstrations, campaign, rally, petition, song, party, note, voters, walk, camp, riot, call, flag, postcard, leader, record, anthem.

_v._ + a storm of protest

provoke, raise, cause, spark.

objection（n.）

❖ 例句

The movie star has no objection to the media taking picture of her family.
這名電影明星不反對媒體拍攝她家人的照片。

❖ 常用搭配詞

adj. + objection

conscientious, strong, main, possible, serious, major, fundamental, same, further, other, formal, obvious, local, real, specific, practical, moral, legal, principal, valid, religious, political, basic, environmental, final, late, reasonable, various, theoretical, chief, related, certain, standard, competent, immediate, official, ideological, ethical, principled, emotional, likely, common, technical, powerful, methodological, initial, strenuous, general, substantial, significant, preliminary, original.

dissent（n.）

❖ 例句

Although voices of dissent were being heard, the government refused to accept Syrian refugees.

雖然一直有反對聲浪，政府還是拒絕接納敘利亞難民。

❖ 常用搭配詞

adj. + dissent

   political, religious, internal, old, radical, rational, open, popular, serious, industrial, individual, moral, further, continuing, growing, increasing, philosophical, social.

n. + of dissent

   voices, forms, intolerance, tradition, cause, repression, murmurs, suppression, memorandum, culture, growth, dissidence, school, expression, displays.

v. + dissent

   indicate, suppress, provoke, cause, show, stifle, encourage, cushion.

綜合整理

protest	言詞或行動的抗議，可能是針對不公平的事、不對的事、或不喜歡的事情，公開的抗議活動屬於此類，後面常接介系詞at或against，後面的名詞通常是事情而不是人。
objection	對某件事情有異議，不贊成，後面常接介系詞to，後面的名詞通常是事情而不是人；也指在法庭上律師覺得另一方律師的說詞不當而表示抗議。
dissent	指不同意政府官方的決定或大家接受的意見，後面很少接介系詞和反對的事情，而是常在前面加介系詞of（如intolerance of dissent不容忍異議等）。

Unit 4 苦難

StringNet語料庫出現次數

distress	misery	hardship	ordeal	adversity	tribulation
1471	1284	835	609	170	92

distress（n.）

❖ 例句

I consider this a monstrous libel and it has caused grave distress to my family and me.

我視此為醜惡的誹謗，它對我和我的家人造成極大的痛苦。

She faced the tragedy with courage even though she was obviously in great distress.

縱然她顯然處在極大的痛苦中，她仍然勇敢地面對這個悲劇。

❖ 常用搭配詞

adj. + distress

great, financial, social, considerable, emotional, psychological, obvious, mental, acute, economic, personal, deep, physical, real, genuine, extreme, immediate, severe, short-term, immense, inner, evident, undue, prolonged, avoidable, national, increasing, intense, resulting.

misery（n.）

❖ 例句

His boss has made his life a misery.
他的老闆使他的生活苦不堪言。

❖ 常用搭配詞

adj. + misery

human, more, untold, much, abject, such, personal, old, economic, sheer, extreme, great, total, mounting, absolute, utter, cold, real, prolonged, intense, deep, emotional.

misery of + n.

unemployment, people, women.

hardship（n.）

❖ 例句

Plunging prices of produce have caused extreme hardship for farmers throughout the Third World.
農產品價格的下跌使第三世界的農夫處境艱困。

❖ 常用搭配詞

<u>v.</u> + adj. + hardship

cause, suffer, experience, face, alleviate, bring, impose.

<u>adj.</u> + hardship

financial, economic, great, severe, real, physical, considerable, suffering, personal, extreme, substantial, unnecessary, social, genuine, immense, appalling, serious, dreadful, exceptional, acute, current, increasing, enormous, terrible.

ordeal（n.）

❖ 例句

Thank God she had been spared the ordeal of surgery.
感謝上帝她不必受開刀之苦。
The family's ordeal began when the fugitive burst into their house.
當那個逃犯闖入他們的家，這家人的惡夢就開始了。

❖ 常用搭配詞

<u>v.</u> + ordeal

spare, face, survive, has, follow.

<u>adj.</u> + ordeal

this, terrible, long, terrify, same, dreadful, horrific, hour-long, three-hour, nerve-jangling, recent, annual, personal.

adversity（n.）

❖ 例句

We will always remember his courage and resilience in the face of adversity.
我們會永遠記得他在逆境中的勇氣和韌性。

綜合整理

distress	指由於缺乏金錢或食物而造成的問題或痛苦，前面動詞常用cause。另外也常用在身體的疾病（例如respiratory distress呼吸窘迫）。
misery	很大的痛苦或困境，例如因為貧病交迫而造成。常用在片語make someone's life a misery（使某人生活苦不堪言）。
hardship	指由於缺乏金錢造成生活上的艱苦。
ordeal	持續一段較短時間的痛苦經驗，如生病等。由於時間較短，且常是因為偶發事件，常用在Someone's ordeal began when...的句型。
adversity	因為不幸、運氣不佳而導致必須面對許多問題。
tribulation	正式用字，指嚴重的問題或困難。

Unit 5 忽視

StringNet語料庫出現次數

ignore	neglect
7066	1351

ignore（vt.）

❖ 常用句型

> **S + ignore + O**
> **S + be（adv.）ignored**

❖ 例句

Scarlet danced and laughed at the party, pretending to ignore the presence of Brad.

Scarlet在派對上跳舞歡笑，假裝無視於Brad的存在。

The strike demand was totally ignored by the dictator.

這個獨裁者完全不理會罷工的訴求。

❖ 常用搭配詞

ignore + the n.

　　fact, possibility, question, advice, role, way, warning, problem, views, rest, reality, issue, needs, existence, effects, importance, extent, interruption, sarcasm, pain, remark, request, influence, interests, principle, plight, rules, evidence, summons, significance, sounds, impact, nature, child, situation, law, risks, look, demands, presence, difference, heat, dog, power, chance, criticism, call, rights, girl, threat, invitation, relationship, matter, feeling, consequences, implication, difficulties.

adv. + ignore

largely, simply, completely, totally, virtually, deliberately, usually, entirely, generally, studiously, easily, conveniently, blithely, widely, always, safely, frequently, consistently, pointedly, determinedly, normally, resolutely, merely, blatantly, apparently, invariably, systematically, wholly, practically.

v. + to ignore

afford, try, choose, decide, continue, pretend.

neglect（vt.）

❖ 常用句型

> **S + be +（adv.）neglected**
> **S + neglect + O**

❖ 例句

The issue of low birth rate had been neglected by the government before its impact on the entire educational system emerged.
政府一直忽視少子化的問題，直到它對教育體系產生衝擊。
The mother was accused of neglecting her 5-year-old child, who had been left alone at home for a week.
這個母親因為把她五歲的孩子獨自留在家中一個禮拜而被起訴忽視親職。

❖ 常用搭配詞

adv. + neglect

largely, sadly, totally, relatively, seriously, entirely, usually, grossly, comparatively, willfully, wrongfully, wholly, completely, conveniently, strangely, deliberately.

neglect+ the n.

fact, child, role, importance, possibility, question, way, cause, material, relationship.

綜合整理

ignore	故意忽略已經被告知或已經知道的事情，或是佯裝沒聽見或看見某人或某事。因為是刻意的，所以前面可以接decide to, choose to 等動詞，也常接deliberately表示故意忽視。
neglect	因為疏忽不注意而沒有好好照顧某個人或做好某件事情，後面的受詞常接child表示沒有好好照顧孩童。也可以當名詞，時常和abuse一起用（abuse and neglect虐待和忽視）。

Unit 6 機靈的，機智的

StringNet語料庫出現次數

clever	smart	shrewd	witty	tactful	resourceful
2361	1554	465	433	166	132

clever（adj.）

❖ 例句

He is clever at getting what he wants.
他很會想辦法得到他要的東西。

❖ 常用搭配詞

clever + n.

girl, boy, man, people, idea, use, way, woman, men, folly, clogs, stuff, things, move, trick, combination, fellow, children, play, lawyers, choice, pass, eyes, plan, device, lass, person, software, fingers, answer, puns, swine, heads, scientist, research, system, mind, wording, gimmick, devil, footballer, wife, twist, concealment, politician.

smart（adj.）

❖ 例句

Don't play smart, kid.
小子，別耍花樣!
She is smart enough to keep her mouth shut.
她很聰明，知道不能把此事說出去。

❖ 常用搭配詞

smart + n.

move, man, people, way, answer, girl, women, guy, fellow, operator, remark, stuff, kid, blow, friends, lawyer, trick, ploy, idea.

shrewd（adj.）

❖ 例句

He is a shrewd man of the world，manipulating the foolishness and greed of people around him.
他是個聰明世故的人，擅長於操弄周遭人的愚蠢與貪婪。

❖ 常用搭配詞

shrewd + n.

opportunist, competitors, politicians, shots, judge, view, man.

witty（adj.）

❖ 例句

The speaker gave a witty and entertaining talk on the customs of Chinese lunar new year.
演講者以詼諧風趣的方式演說有關中國農曆新年的習俗。

❖ 常用搭配詞

witty and + adj.

amusing, entertaining, colorful, original, imaginative.

witty + n.

articles, style, account, conversation, works, books, juxtapositions, scripts, women, ad, twist, numbers, performance, comedy, remarks.

tactful（adj.）

❖ 例句

She tried to think of a tactful way of stating the brutal truth.
她嘗試用比較不傷感情的方式來說出這個殘酷的事實。

❖ 常用搭配詞

tactful + n.

way, questioning, silence, retreat, approach, explanation, handling.

resourceful（adj.）

❖ 例句

Always a resourceful woman，Lucy knew she would come up with the solution.

Lucy 一直是個足智多謀的女性，她知道自己一定會找到解決之道。

❖ 常用搭配詞

resourceful + n.

woman, way, lady, housewives.

綜合整理

clever	善於察覺狀況，用聰明才智甚至不誠實的手段來達到目的。另外也表示擅長做某事（be clever at + Ving）或形容事物很巧妙。後面接的名詞可以是人或非人。
smart	機靈、耍小聰明（play smart）。此字主要意義為聰明、明智的，現在時常用來表示智慧型的科技產品（如smart house智慧型房屋）。後面接的名詞可以是人或非人。
shrewd	善於判斷情勢和人，常用來形容和商業有關的人或事（如shrewd businessman機靈的商人, shrewd investment聰明的投資）。後面接的名詞可以是人或非人。
witty	說話機智而幽默，常和其他形容詞一起用（如witty and ironic詼諧而諷刺的），後面修飾的名詞通常不是人。
tactful	說話或做事機智謹慎，以致於不會得罪他人或使他人尷尬，後面接的名詞很少是人。
resourceful	足智多謀，很會想辦法解決實際問題。另外也指資源豐富的。後面接的名詞通常是人。

補充：a nimble mind/brain表示機智的，能夠快速理解或策畫事情。單獨nimble表示行動靈活敏捷的。

Unit 7 機警的

StringNet語料庫出現次數

alert	watchful	vigilant	observant
1145	271	207	134

alert（adj.）

❖ 例句

Psychiatrists should be alert to the possibilities of a patient losing all hope.

心理醫師應該要注意病人失去所有盼望的可能性。

❖ 常用搭配詞

be alert to the + n.

  possibility, advantage, danger.

alert + n.

  expression, system, mind, levels, eyes, reader, interest, opponent,
  status, neighbor, intelligence, state, attention, hits, management, referee,
  manner, driver.

v. + alert

  stay, look, keep, become, remain,

adv. + alert

more, mentally, most, suddenly, immediately, constantly, instantly, sufficiently, continuously.

watchful（adj.）

❖ 例句

Nancy sat on the porch keeping watchful on her children, who were playing in the yard.

Nancy 坐在門廊上，同時注意她的孩子們在院子玩耍。

❖ 常用搭配詞

watchful + n.

eye, waiting, gaze, look, face, silence.

vigilant（adj.）

❖ 例句

There have been several break-ins in our neighborhood and we are all warned to be vigilant.

我們家附近最近有幾起闖空門事件，我們被告知要小心。

❖ 常用搭配詞

v. + vigilant

remain.

adv. + vigilant
extra, constantly, particularly, specially.

vigilant + n.
neighbor, method, eyes.

observant（adj.）

❖ 例句

His secretary is highly observant, good at noticing things.
他的秘書觀察入微，善於察覺異狀。

❖ 常用搭配詞

observant + n.
eye, man, reader, Jews, member, onlooker, person.

adv. + observant
acutely, fairly.

綜合整理

alert	注意周遭環境，專注且反應快，隨時準備行動（如stay alert保持警覺）。
watchful	注意周遭環境以免事情出錯。後面名詞很少是人，常用在片語keep a watchful eye監視，以及under the watchful eyes of someone（在某人的監視之下）。
vigilant	注意周遭環境以察覺危險、錯誤或不法之事。
observant	善於觀察，後面名詞時常是人，描述人的個性機警。另外也指服從法律或信仰規範的。
補充：sharp表示反應快，不易上當。在語料庫出現次數多，但是大部分表示其他多種意義，最常表示尖銳的，鋒利的，因此不列入本項。	

Unit 8 即席，即興的

StringNet語料庫出現次數

impromptu	improvised
148	115

impromptu（adj.）

❖ 例句

He won the first place in the English impromptu speech contest.
她在這場英文即席演講中獲得第一名。

❖ 常用搭配詞

impromptu + n.

　press conference, lecture, speech, performance, concert, meeting, picknic, break, wedding, action,

improvised（vi./vt.）

❖ 例句

The mayor forgot his note of speech, so he had to improvise.
市長忘記帶他的演講稿，所以必須即席演講。

❖ 常用搭配詞

improvised + n.

　drama, state, platform, music, prayers, shelter, material, response.

綜合整理

impromptu	未經計劃或準備就去做一件事情或發表演講，也可以當名詞和副詞。
improvised	從動詞improvise而來，也表示未準備就去做一件事情，但是由於迫於臨時的需要；也指將就湊合材料做成某個東西（如improvised shelter）；另外也表示即興創作（音樂或文章等）（如improvised music）。

Unit 9 家庭

StringNet語料庫出現次數

house	family	home	household
57526	41658	37990	5623

house（n.）

❖ 例句

The former President was placed under house arrest for three years.

這位總統曾被軟禁三年。

He ran a guest house.

他經營一家民宿（小型賓館）。

❖ 常用搭配詞

adj. + house

new, old, own, big, lower, whole, upper, terraced, little, great, private, large, small, empty, Victorian, detached, safe, historic, main, beautiful, halfway, fine, modern, lovely, wooden, rented, haunted, present, original, good, bedroomed, suburban, neighboring, ordinary, thatched, single, eighteenth-century, two-story, comfortable, entire, timber-framed, adjoining, grand, green, three-bedroomed, attractive, elegant, converted, red-brick, middle-class, deserted, local, furnished, back-to-back, suitable, owner-occupied, spacious, traditional, warm, aristocratic, handsome, damp, splendid, vacant, decent, shabby, 15-member, magnificent, circular, unoccupied.

n. + house

country, guest, town, boarding, mansion, stone, acid, dwelling, coffee, mill, family, lodging, moat, terrace, brick, summer, hill, farm, corner, parker, engine, glass, custom, bedroom, boat, coach, sea, community, eating, tree, beach, wood, animal, street, dream, heartbreak, slaughter, rest, village, sugar, store, holiday, tea, prison, ranch.

family（n.）

❖ 例句

More and more children are growing up in single-parent families.
越來越多小孩在單親家庭中成長。

❖ 常用搭配詞

adj. + family

whole, large, extended, local, happy, young, poor, small, one-parent, average, single-parent, entire, working-class, big, noble, homeless, individual, normal, wealthy, British, traditional, Jewish, natural, low-income, Christian, foster, joint, human, real, ordinary, bourgeois, private, strong, aristocratic, ancient, two-parent, bereaved, modern, landed, nice, loving, grieving, rural, affected, typical, two-child, stable, adoptive, immigrant, conventional, respectable, heterosexual, distinguished, rich, broken, conjugal, orthodox, permanent, devoted, intimate, original, stricken, divided, domestic, supportive, warm, prosperous, rival, ideal, religious, well-known, unemployed, fatherless.

family + n.

life, members, planning, size, health, business, history, relationships, allowances, doctor, income, unit, man, law, name, firm, support, network, holiday, connections, background, tradition, responsibilities, expenditure, structure, division, reunion, problems, ties, car, house, situation, home, therapy, care, circle, commitments, values, circumstances, welfare, affair, farm, matters, atmosphere, fortunes, entertainment, formation, economy, breakdown, pride, property, estate, relations, pet, types, resemblance, trust, environment, gathering, budget, vault, photographs, outing, portraits, time, line, feud, finances, influence, loyalty, bond, motto, events, crisis, tragedy, likeness, jewels, conflict, disputes.

home（n.）

❖ 例句

Here we are again, home sweet home.
又回到家了！金窩，銀窩，不如自己的狗窩。

❖ 常用搭配詞

adj. +home

own, residential, matrimonial, nursing, stately, private, ideal, Scottish, old, permanent, foster, mobile, spiritual, ancestral, broken, parental, real, natural, luxury, convalescent, comfortable, happy, temporary, present, previous, original, traditional, proper, safe, secure, empty, average, sweet, suitable, working-class, marital, successive, late, stable, future, nice, modern, affordable, mental, true, unbeaten, large, small, loving, beautiful, final, local, voluntary, terraced, low-cast, substitute, Christian, perfect, adopted, labor, modest, rural, detached, respective, registered, ordinary, humble, conservative, Jewish, separate, normal, elegant, enhanced, sheltered, guaranteed, simple, deprived, regular.

home + n.

town, care, affairs, side, help, rule, game, ownership, life, ground, owners, country, guard, address, environment, economics, support, territory, visits, unions, farm, stores, village, cooking, service, defence, city, telephone, circumstances, management, background, consumption, insurance, member, furnishings, movie, responsibilities, workers, clash, decorating, comforts, income, safety, health.

household（n.）

❖ 例句

The general household survey is a continuous nation survey of people living in private household.

戶口普查是調查住在私人住戶人口的持續的全國性調查。

❖ 常用搭配詞

adj. + household

royal, average, own, private, concealed, single-person, British, large, low-income, ordinary, domestic, individual, elderly, small, whole, poor, rural, normal, younger, similar, total, independent, joint, single, separate, three-generational, durable, shared, extended, selected, wealthy, local, two-parent, entire, common, nuclear, parental, noble, essential, working-class, care-giving, homeless, aristocratic, non-family, multi-family, respective, typical, complex, lone.

household + <u>n.</u>

survey, goods, name, waste, size, income, chores, items, tasks, appliances, formation, contents, rubbish, products, bills, management, expenses, structure, budget, members, composition, duties, cleaning, accounts, objects, types, insurance, refuse, chemicals, expenditure, furniture, head, bleach, work, economy, equipment, pets, characteristics, resources, servants, division, utensils, men, type, policy, finances, articles, consumption, services, maintenance, needs, furnishings, savings, cleaners, tax.

綜合整理

house	住家，給人居住的建築物，尤其指獨棟一樓或獨棟多層樓的透天厝。另外也表示機構、議院、劇場等特殊目的的建築物。前面接的形容詞和名詞多半形容房子的建材、位置、用途、構造、或狀況等。例如a warm house表示房子的外觀或擺設給人溫馨的感覺。
family	有血緣關係的人組成的家庭。前面接的形容詞多半描述家庭成員的狀況、屬性、或關係等。例如a warm family指家人關係親密。前面不常接名詞，後面則經常接名詞。
home	一個人自幼成長的家庭，強調有安全感或歸屬感（如home town家鄉）。也指某人或某家庭定居的住處，包含獨棟房屋和公寓大樓，或提供醫療照護的機構（如nursing home安養院）。前面不常接名詞，後面經常接名詞。
household	住在同一間房子的人，一戶家庭，包括僕人。前面常接形容詞表示住戶的狀況（如multi-family household有二個家庭構成的一戶人家）。後面常接名詞表示和居家住戶有關的人事物（例如household head家長，household appliances家電）。

Unit 10 艱難的，費力的

StringNet語料庫出現次數

strenuous	arduous	laborious
305	241	189

strenuous（adj.）

❖ 例句

It was quite a strenuous walk— the path rising in zigzags up the hillside for a hundred yards or so.

走這條路很費力，因為它沿著之字形上坡約一百碼左右。

The university made strenuous efforts to upgrade the computing facilities on campus.

這所大學盡全力把全校的電腦設備升級。

❖ 常用搭配詞

strenuous + n.

efforts, exercise, attempts, opposition, activity, walk, objections, hike, program, business, job, route, action, tasks, management, life, part, work, days, climb.

arduous（adj.）

❖ 例句

They began the arduous task of carrying the plants downstairs.
他們開始搬盆栽下樓的艱難任務。

❖ 常用搭配詞

arduous + n.

   task, work, journey, climb, conditions, process, trek, battle, voyage, business, hours, rut, training, duties, life, part, effort, negotiations.

laborious（adj.）

❖ 例句

Waxing is a very laborious process and the wood will require re-waxing at regular intervals.
打蠟是很耗工費時的程序，而且木頭（地板）每隔一段時間又必須重新打蠟。

❖ 常用搭配詞

laborious + n.

   process, business, task, method, way, job, system, employment, hand, work.

綜合整理

strenuous	艱苦繁重的，需要耗費許多力量或努力。另外也指積極的。
arduous	費力的，也指山坡等難攀登或陡峭的。
laborious	費時且費力的。

Unit 11 堅持

StringNet語料庫出現次數

insist	assert	persist	persevere
6507	2052	1759	179

insist（vi.）

❖ 常用句型

> S + insist on N/ Ving
> S + insist that + S（should）do something

❖ 例句

He insisted that he was innocent.

他堅稱自己是無辜的。

She insisted on seeing the picture even though she was afraid.

縱然她很害怕，她還是堅持要看那張照片。

❖ 常用搭配詞

insist on + Ving

　taking, having, going, seeing, coming, calling, doing, using, making, paying, giving, playing, wearing, keeping, retaining, telling, putting, driving, receiving, staying, accompanying, getting, buying, moving, treating, remaining, returning, looking, carrying, helping, walking, showing, maintaining, waiting, hearing, standing, marrying, travelling, bringing, cooking, knowing, meeting, selling, trying, collecting, climbing, checking, visiting, continuing, speaking, following, dragging, saying, serving, stopping, inspecting, pursuing, cutting.

adv. + insist

also, still, always, often, only, again, later, probably, usually, even , repeatedly, rightly, previously, stubbornly, nevertheless, normally, actually, absolutely, really, continually, recently, reportedly, frequently, increasingly, quietly, invariably, immediately, successful, merely, constantly, properly, originally, wisely, impiously.

assert（vt.）

❖ 常用句型

> **S + assert + O**

❖ 例句

The President asserted that direct action was the only way to deal with terrorist countries.
總統堅持對付恐怖主義國家的唯一方法就是直接行動。
In his book, the writer asserts the existence of space aliens.
作者在他的書中斷定外星人的確存在。

❖ 常用搭配詞

assert the + n.
   primacy, right, existence, dignity, need.

adv. + assert

also, often, explicitly, confidently, simply, merely, still, further, frequently, successfully, directly, repeatedly, strongly, regularly, continually, commonly, positively, again, openly, always, gradually, boldly, constantly, emphatically, rightly, firmly, apparently, falsely.

persist（vi.）

❖ 常用句型

> **S + persist（in Ving/N）**
> **S + persist with +N**

❖ 例句

If your symptoms persist for more than a few days , contact your doctor for advice.

如果再過幾天你的症狀還繼續就要去看醫生。

The famous singer persisted in denying his relationship with his new assistant.

那位有名的歌手不斷否認和他的新助理有戀情。

❖ 常用搭配詞

persist in + Ving

trying, using, calling, believing, making, wearing, taking, going, pursuing, interpreting, maintaining, giving, looking, seeing, offering, keeping, applying, advocating, talking, pressing, dragging, denying, arguing, preferring.

adv. + persist

still, nevertheless, also, often, stubbornly, usually, then, even, probably, doggedly.

persevere（vi.）

❖ 常用句型

S + persevere in Ving/N
S + persevere with +N

❖ 例句

He persevered with his invention for many years.
有好幾年的時間他埋頭苦幹於他的發明。

❖ 常用搭配詞

persevere with + n.

game, task, robot, attempt.

綜合整理

insist	堅持某件事情的真實性，尤其是別人不相信的時候，也指堅持要讓某件事情發生，包含自己要做某件事情或要某個人做某件事情。
assert	堅持某件事情的真實性，也指堅持自己的權利、意見、立場等，主詞通常是人或書等文件。
persist	持續地去做一件事情，尤其是別人反對或遇到困難的時候；也指病情等負面現象持續存在不消退。語料庫中persist後面的介系詞通常是in，幾乎沒有with。
persevere	堅定不畏困難地持續去做一件事情，有正面意義。主詞是人，通常不和副詞一起出現。

Unit 12 減少，降低

StringNet語料庫出現次數

reduce	decline	decrease	diminish	lessen	dwindle
17644	4092	1625	1376	491	276

reduce（vt.）

❖ 常用句型

> S + reduce + O（by + N）+（to + N）
> S + reduce + O from N to N

❖ 例句

This change has severely reduced the amount of pension that many pensioners receive.

這個改變已經大幅降低領退休金的人實際領到的金額。

Overall mortality and cardiovascular mortality were reduced by 20% to 25% in patients randomized to an exercise program.

針對參加一項運動計畫的病人的隨機調查，整體死亡率及心血管死亡率降低了百分之二十，來到百分之二十五。

Compulsory military service in Spain was reduced from 12 to nine months from Jan. 1 , 1992.

從1992年一月一日起西班牙的義務兵役時間從12個月降到9個月。

❖ 常用搭配詞

reduce the + n.

　　number, amount, risk, size, cost, need, level, likelihood, incidence, time, rate, power, price, value, deficit, impact, demand, budget, possibility, volume, heat, use, ability, scope, burden, extent, frequency, role, quantity, proportion, pressure, length, flow, chance, problem, effectiveness, effect, degree, potential, importance, noise, influence, tax, danger, supply, gap, scale, range, damage, tension, weight, quality, speed, temperature, threat, strength, severity, dose, income, share, workload, distance, capital, debt, uncertainty, workforce, dependence, complexity, tendency, incentive, unemployment, ambiguity, output, depth, stock, pitch, production, angle, spread, opportunity, loss, intake, space, suffering, growth, emission.

adv. + reduce

　　substantially, significantly, greatly, considerably, drastically, further, dramatically, slightly, sharply, gradually, severely, actually, progressively, seriously, vastly, somewhat, steadily, eventually, effectively, correspondingly, markedly, largely, massively, strongly, heavily, successively, profoundly, systematically, sufficiently, entirely, slowly.

decrease（vi./vt.）

❖ 常用句型

> **S + decrease（+ O）（to/by/from/with + N）**

❖ 例句

The total forest cover of the Earth is decreasing.
地球的森林面積正在減少。

Crime has decreased by 70 percent since the cameras were installed.
自從架設攝影機以後，犯罪事件減少了百分之七十。

The error rate decreases with practice.
犯錯率隨著練習的增加而遞減。

The food you eat can increase or decrease your risk of heart disease and stroke.
你吃的食物可以提高或減低心臟病和中風的風險。

❖ 常用搭配詞

（det.） n. + decrease

  temperature, rate, cost, system, size, population, speed, mortality, energy, frequency, range, quality, consumption, volume, distance, influence, concentration, radiation, length, deviation, product.

decrease with + n.

  age, time, distance, depth.

decrease + the n.

  amount, danger, demand, ratio, rate.

decrease + adv.

  significantly, rapidly, steadily, markedly, slightly, further, dramatically, accordingly, considerably, substantially, linearly, smoothly, proportionally, stepwise, gradually, sharply, roughly.

decline（vi.）

❖ 常用句型

> **S + decline（+ prep. + N）**

❖ 例句

The sales of hybrid cars have declined by 10 percent.
油電混合汽車的銷售量減少了百分之十。

❖ 常用搭配詞

（det.） n. + decline

sales, membership, production, right, rate, business, population, growth, employment, profits, prices, share, trade, use, consumption, births, goods, wages, trust, employment, output, influence, number.

diminish（vi./vt.）

❖ 常用句型

> **S + diminish（+ O）**

❖ 例句

The fact that Jack had a mistress didn't diminish the affection he had for his wife.
Jack 有情婦的事實並未減少他對她妻子的感情。

In Australia , at least 30 species of frogs are diminishing.
在澳洲，至少有30種青蛙數量正在減少當中。

❖ 常用搭配詞

diminish + the n.

  importance, need, power, number, role, authority, amount, influence, impact, quality, value, status, effect, usefulness, degree, independence, ability, extent, contribution, size, willingness, credibility, significance, ardor, pleasure.

 adv. + diminish

  gradually, greatly, steadily, seriously, significantly, further, severely, rapidly, considerably, somehow, progressively, sharply, actually, substantially, surely, slowly, inevitably, automatically, gratuitously, necessarily, constantly, accordingly, unduly, gravely, clearly, normally.

lessen（vi./vt.）

❖ 常用句型

S + lesson（+ O）

❖ 例句

Visual fatigue can be lessened by closing the eyes for a minute or two.
閉上眼睛一、二分鐘可以減輕視力疲勞。

The need for legal help for poor people has lessened in recent years.
近年來貧窮人對於法律協助的需求已經降低。

❖ 常用搭配詞

lesson + the _n._

   risk, chances, impact, burden, need, likelihood, effects, possibility, pressure, amount, pain, disadvantages, temptation, tensions, degree, importance, danger, gap, distance, problem, role, significance, attractiveness, flow.

adv. + lessen

   gradually, never, considerably, significantly, actually, thereby, greatly, already, urgently, least.

dwindle（vi.）

❖ 常用句型

> **S + dwindle（away）**
> **S + dwindle to + N**

❖ 例句

The polar bear population has been dwindling.

北極熊的數量一直在減少。

His class of fifty students dwindled to fifteen.

他班上的學生從五十人逐漸減少到十五人。

❖ 常用搭配詞

（det.）_n._ + dwindle

numbers, fortunes, attendance, support, business, population.

dwindle to +（det.）adj.+ _n._

trickle, point, size.

dwindle in + _n._

number, importance, consequence.

綜合整理

reduce	及物動詞。減少大小、數量、及價格。
decline	不及物動詞。除了減少的意義，還表示拒絕和變差的意思，因此在語料庫出現的次數多。
decrease	及物或不及物動詞。數量減少或程度降低。在語料庫中較常當作不及物動詞。
diminish	及物或不及物動詞。變少或變小，和reduce相似。
lesson	及物或不及物動詞。減少大小、重要性、或價值，和reduce相似。也可以表示減輕疼痛等感覺。
dwindle	不及物動詞。逐漸變少或變小。

Unit 13 減輕

StringNet語料庫出現次數

alleviate	subside	lighten	mitigate	abate
547	458	306	291	211

alleviate（vt.）

❖ 常用句型

> **S + alleviate + O**

❖ 例句

Tax increase is considered a way to alleviating domestic economic difficulties.
增加賦稅被視為減輕國內經濟問題的一種方法。

❖ 常用搭配詞

alleviate +（the）n.

problem, unemployment, symptoms, situation, suffering, plight, effects, pain, burden, shortage, stress, tax, crisis, impact, traffic, pressure, debt, anxiety, famine, things, concerns, tension, position.

subside（vi.）

❖ 常用句型

S + subside

❖ 例句

The singer waited until the applause subsided and started the next song.
那位歌手等掌聲平靜下來然後開始唱下一首歌曲。

❖ 常用搭配詞

（det.）n. + subside

anger, pain, noise, tears, storm, subs, laughter, symptom, flood, demonstration, convulsions, panic, fuss, wind.

lighten（vt.）

❖ 常用句型

S + lighten + O

❖ 例句

The magnificent donation has lightened the financial worries of this orphanage.
這筆鉅額款減輕了這間孤兒院的財務煩惱。

❖ 常用搭配詞

lighten + the n.

  atmosphere, tension, load, burden.

mitigate（vt.）

❖ 常用句型

> **S+ mitigate + O**

❖ 例句

Forests play a key role in mitigating the greenhouse effect by soaking up carbon dioxide.

樹林能夠吸收二氧化碳，因此在減經溫室效應上扮演關鍵的角色。

❖ 常用搭配詞

mitigate + the n.

  greenhouse effects, tedium, offence, problem, amount, need.

abate（vi./vt.）

❖ 常用句型

> **S +abate（+ O）**

❖ 例句

The next day the fever abated and she began to recover.
第二天她的燒退了而且開始康復。

❖ 常用搭配詞

（det.）_n._ +abate
　storm, wind, anxiety.

abate +（det.）_n._
　odor, nuisance.

綜合整理

alleviate	減輕痛苦的程度或處理的困難度，受詞通常有負面意義的名詞（如壓力、債務等）。
subside	逐漸減輕、消退，以至於停止或平靜。主詞時常是感覺（如疼痛）、聲音、或劇烈的氣候（如洪水）。另外也指建築物等下沉。
lighten	減輕工作量、憂慮、或債務等。緩和凝重或悲傷的氣氛。另有其他意義，如照亮，變淡等，因此在語料庫表示減輕的例子不多。
mitigate	正式用字，減輕某個負面因素的影響力或嚴重程度，使其令人不愉快或傷害程度降低。
abate	正式用字，減弱，平息。主詞時常是猛烈的氣候（如暴風雨）、人的情緒（如怒氣）、或是疾病（如發燒）等。

Unit 14 謹慎的

StringNet語料庫出現次數

careful	cautious	wary	discreet	prudent	meticulous	scrupulous	fastidious	circumspect
5044	1099	791	526	486	284	131	109	85

careful（adj.）

❖ 常用句型

> **S + be careful（not to do something）**
> **S + be careful about +N**

❖ 例句

We should be careful not to fall into the trap.
我們應該要小心不要掉入陷阱。
Be careful what you say.
小心你所說的話（以免說錯話）。

❖ 常用搭配詞

should/must be careful not to + Vroot
　　make, give, confuse, let, assume.

careful + n.
　　consideration, attention, planning, thought, analysis, study, examination,
　　note, selection, preparation, management, scrutiny, handling, look,

reading, eye, assessment, watch, design, control, aim, supervision, searching, drafting, way, work, training, timing, questioning, hands, measurement, second, organization, speech, definition, manipulation, observer, man, avoidance, calculation, distance, screening, diplomacy, driver, voice, precautions, movement.

cautious（adj.）

❖ 常用句型

> **S + be cautious about + Ving**

❖ 例句

He is cautious about getting involved in a relationship.
他對於感情非常謹慎。

❖ 常用搭配詞

be cautious about + Ving
  interpreting, giving, taking, allowing, making, getting.

cautious + n.
  approach, welcome, optimism, attitude, man, policy, line, side, response, look, nature, glance, note, conjectures, experimentation, eye, smile, king, sip, lenders, organization, words, trading, pragmatism, opening, step, approval, program, outlook, support, start, assumption, interest, way, search, voice, account, budget, moves, conclusion, hypotheses.

wary（adj.）

❖ 常用句型

> **S + be wary of（+ Ving）**

❖ 例句

He has been wary of placing too much trust in her.
他一直小心不要太信任她。
Be wary of judging people by their wealth.
小心不要用財富來評斷他人。

❖ 常用搭配詞

be wary of + Ving

　　making, accepting, placing, doing, using, giving, claiming, going, asking, creating, upsetting, becoming, putting, allowing, taking.

wary + n.

　　fox, respect, glance, politeness.

discreet（adj）.

❖ 常用句型

> **S + be discreet（about +N）**

❖ 例句

They are pretty open with each other but very discreet outside.
他們對彼此很開放，但是在外面就非常謹言慎行。
He was discreet about his sex with his mistress and she left his room in the early dawn.
他對於和情婦的偷情很小心，她天一亮就離開他的房間。

❖ 常用搭配詞

discreet + n.

  distance, enquiries, way, side, gestures, discussions, gentility, contacts, notice, cough.

v. + discreet + n.

  ask / questions, hold / discussions, make / contact, make / enquiries, provide / support.

prudent（adj.）

❖ 常用句型

It（modal v）+ be prudent to do something

❖ 例句

It would be prudent to have your cholesterol tested by your doctor.
你還是去給醫生檢查膽固醇比較保險。

❖ 常用搭配詞

be prudent to + <u>Vroot</u>

　　have, keep, leave, do , consider, make, assume, confirm, take, discuss.

prudent + <u>n.</u>

　　management, man, manner, use, liquidity, investment, course, ratio, employer, marriage, step, action, way, producer, lender, program, decision, business, housekeeping, budgeting, act, allowance, accounting, tactic, diet, person.

meticulous（adj.）

❖ 常用句型

> **S + be meticulous（in/about +N）**

❖ 例句

The track of the sound reproduction was transferred from original tapes with meticulous care.

這次的原音重現每個音軌都是從原本的母帶極度小心轉錄而成。

She is meticulous in her choice of words.

她用字非常謹慎。

❖ 常用搭配詞

meticulous + <u>n.</u>

　　care, detail, attention, planning, work, research, preparation, scrutiny, observation, organization, craftsmanship, observance, order, approach.

scrupulous（adj.）

❖ 常用句型

S + be scrupulous in/about（Ving）+N

❖ 例句

She is scrupulous in keeping her bedroom tidy.
她非常注重保持她臥室的整潔。
He drew the machine with scrupulous precision.
他精準地畫出那台機器。

❖ 常用搭配詞

scrupulous + _n._

attention, care, adherence, honesty, members, hygiene, fairness, precision, characters.

fastidious（adj.）

❖ 常用句型

S + be fastidious about/in +N

❖ 例句

She is fastidious about her hairstyle.
她極度注意她的髮型。

❖ 常用搭配詞

fastidious + n.

members, taste, customers, detail, concern, manner.

circumspect（adj.）

❖ 常用句型

> **S + be circumspect（in +N/ Ving）**

❖ 例句

He must be very circumspect in avoiding covetousness.
他必須謹慎小心以免引起別人貪念。

❖ 常用搭配詞

be circumspect in + Ving

appearing, offering, identifying, avoiding, making, discussing.

綜合整理

careful	謹慎小心以避免危險、犯錯、或造成損失。常用在should/ must be careful not to + Vroot以表示警戒。後面接的名詞可以是行動、人、表情、或抽象名詞等。
cautious	因為不確定結果而謹慎保守不冒險，以避免傷害或危險。常用在be cautious about + N/ Ving。後面直接接名詞時，該名詞可以是態度或看法（如welcome, conjecture, approval），行動（如approach, step, glance），表情（如smile, eye），或是人（如king, man）。
wary	保持警覺，注意危險發生。常用在句型be wary of + N/ Ving，而較少在wary後面接名詞，如果有也很少是人。此字本身有提防的意思，比較：Be wary of putting too much trust in him. = Be careful not to put too much trust in him.
discreet	謹言慎行，考慮週到，以免冒犯他人或被發現。另外也表示不引人注意的。後面接的名詞很少是人。
prudent	做事慎思明辨，避免風險（如a prudent investment謹慎的投資），後面接的名詞可以是人或非人。
meticulous	過度謹慎，拘泥細節。
scrupulous	謹慎周全以求精確。
fastidious	非常注意細節，近乎吹毛求疵，常用在句型be fastidious about + N。
circumspect	密切注意周遭環境，審慎評估後果後才採取行動。後面很少接名詞。

Unit 15 競賽，競爭，比賽

StringNet語料庫出現次數

game	competition	match	tournament	contest
20607	10064	8918	2066	1690

game（n.）

❖ 例句

He turned down the party invitation to see his boy at a baseball game.
他拒絕了那個派對的邀約而去看他兒子參加棒球比賽。

❖ 常用搭配詞

n. + game

home, (rugby) league, ball, opening, (golden) cup, football, team, championship, adventure, guessing, chess, poker, qualifying, war, world, tennis, rugby, cricket, baseball, winter, warm-up, golf, hunting, army, brain, trophy, soccer, field, race, spelling, driving, boxing.

competition（n.）

❖ 例句

These shops on the street are in fierce competition with each other.
這條街的商店彼此競爭很激烈。

Some karate competitions now include a random drug test.
現在有些空手道會進行隨機藥物抽驗。

❖ 常用搭配詞

adj. + competition

international, this, perfect, direct, increased, foreign, fierce, that, intense, unfair, national, European, stiff, effective, free, fair, open, increasing, global, tough, serious, Japanese, economic, overseas, growing, male, keen, annual, domestic, potential, main, local, severe, aggressive, commercial, healthy, exclusive, proper, exciting, actual, hot, intergroup, qualifying, public, one-day, successful, significant, industrial, future, vigorous, internal, worldwide, outside, cut-throat, dynamic, fabulous, extra, heavy, individual, intrasexual, external, friendly, regional, official, private.

competition + n.

policy, rules, law, authorities, act, winners, commissioner, results, winner, entry, assay, organizer, issues, prize, directorate, tribunal, game, hotline, address, area, time, designs, matters, conditions, model, legislation, question, cases, experiments, line, judges, circuit, table, grounds, system, sports, standards, details, opportunities, match, sponsors, worries, entrants, schemes, leaflets.

n. + competition

cup, price, year, market, UK, caption, party, Liverpool, art, talent, painting, knock-out, football, story, response, essay, piano, karate, stableford, cricket, league, design, world, music, team, quiz, photo, weekend, industry, poetry, beauty, elite, community, village, award, photomicrography, echo, nations, medal, golf, knitting, coloring, business, tennis, poster, writing, bowling, card, season, fashion, darts, photography, trade, newspaper, drama, shooting, hike, prize, invention, baby, debating, carving, innovation, trophy, school.

match（n.）

❖ 例句

The player was suspended for five matches by UEFA after his verbal attack on a British referee.

這位選手因為以言詞攻擊一位英國裁判被禁賽五場。

❖ 常用搭配詞

n. + match

football, league, test, cup, home, opening, championship, cricket, rugby, boxing, division, charity, qualifying, derby, group, return, club, polo, challenge, soccer, county, tennis, exhibition, wrestling, university, world, team, trophy, revenge, trial, debut, warm-up, first-round, pool, golf, day, night, combination, school, basketball, hockey, quarter-final, fishing, celebrity, comeback, semi-final, marathon.

adj. + match

first, this, two, three, last, final, international, round, next, one-day, friendly, important, competitive, close, televised, annual, European, previous, fourth, successive, remaining, tough, single, semi-final, consecutive, exciting, entire, subsequent.

tournament（n.）

❖ 例句

More than 100 golfers from all the country are competing this weekend in Golf Tournament.

來自全國超過100位高爾夫球選手將在本周末的高爾夫球錦標賽中一較高下。

❖ 常用搭配詞

adj. + tournament

this, qualifying, first, sevens, international, major, indoor, royal, five-a-side, whole, open, sterling, great, professional, annual, one-day, triangular, Asian, main, big, national, European, classic, inaugural, recent, competitive, previous, unique, modern, full, quadrangular, under-16, amateur, successful, junior, prestigious, pre-season, toughest, favorite, sponsored.

n. + tournament

golf, tennis, cup, football, soccer, hockey, world, squash, cricket, slam, (hard)court, commonwealth, snooker, bowling, masters, knockout, ratings, invitation, trophy, ranking, service, club, nations, chess, satellite, singles, darts, merit, youth, Chicago, rugby, circuit, memorial, four-nations, volleyball.

contest（n.）

❖ 例句

She has been to a beauty contest in her hometown.
她在家鄉曾經參加選美比賽。

❖ 常用搭配詞

n. + contest

leadership, song, beauty, year, talent, video, republican, investiture, election, nomination, world, run-off, week, grading, eating, lookalike, popularity, band, fishing, opening, universe, cup, writing, baby, word, boxing, championship.

adj. + contest

this, presidential, close, unequal, sporting, good, fair, new, national, open, final, one-sided, thrilling, literary, first, real, international, great, fascinating, political, global, valuable, direct, 1992, equal, military, photographic, arm-wrestling, non-binding, significant, bridal, local, successful, hard-fought, bruising, driving, super, hopeless, 10-round, protracted, primary, bitter, competitive, technical, closing, prestigious, parliamentary, severe, professional.

綜合整理

game	1.運動或遊戲等競賽活動。2.複數games指一系列有組織的體育賽事（如the Olympic Games）。3.一盤（Match）（如網球賽或橋牌比賽）的一局。
competition	1.為爭奪獎品或利益的競爭行為（如economic competition經濟競爭），前面常接形容詞表示競爭的激烈程度（如cut-throat competition割喉戰）或性質（如fair competition公平競爭）。2.技巧或能力的競賽，前面常接各項才藝名詞（如karate, photo, music, writing等），比賽規模及範圍較大（如global competition全球競賽, European competition歐洲競賽）。
match	1.兩個運動隊伍或兩個運動選手的對抗賽，如橄欖球或網球比賽。2.網球比賽的一盤。
tournament	體育錦標賽，聯賽，由許多場比賽組成，由最後積分最高或贏得總決賽的選手得獎，最常用在高爾夫球比賽和網球賽。
contest	1.為了決定優劣勝負的競爭行為（如leadership contest領導地位競爭，military contest軍事競賽）。2.參賽者分開表現能力或技巧，並由評審評分的比賽，前面較少是運動名稱，較多才藝比賽、選美、角逐總統選舉等名詞。

Unit 16 獎品，獎金

StringNet語料庫出現次數

award	prize	reward	bonus	medal	trophy
11497	4071	2721	1764	1603	1584

award（n.）

❖ 例句

Students may undertake full-time supervised research leading to the award of a Ph.D.

學生可以從事有指導教授的全職研究而獲取博士學位的授與。

The actor won an Academy Award for his exceptional performance in the classic musical.

這男演員在這部古典音樂劇演出卓越因此獲得奧斯卡金像獎。

❖ 常用搭配詞

award for + n.

export, services, innovation, excellence, industry, architecture, energy, research, employee, bravery, compensation.

（det.）n. + award

date, (player of the) year, gold, match, group, service, quality, (reader of the) month, pay, academy, safety, arbitration, design, merit, trust, BAFTA, bronze, team, enterprise, actor, penalty, bravery, business, environment, society, training, silver, credit, achievement, player, memorial, innovation, leadership, industry, enclosure, play, council, compensation, practitioner, student, magazine, science, art, portrait.

v. + an award

win, receive, get, make, give, obtain, deserve, present, uphold, accept, gain.

prize（n.）

❖ 例句

Salam and Weinberg were awarded the Nobel prize for physics in 1979.
Salam 和 Weinberg 於1979年獲頒諾貝爾物理獎。
He won the NT$500,000 first prize in the "Young Film Critic of the Year" Competition.
他贏得價值台幣五十萬元的年度青年影評首獎。

❖ 常用搭配詞

n. + prize

Nobel, peace, cash, booker, consolation, turner, raffle, star, letter, book, team, runner-up, Pulitzer, memorial, bonus, £10, school, year, music, record, jury, group, section, holiday, poetry, essay, show, jackpot, break, second, economics, fiction, category, radio, geography, nurse, race, literature, handicap, reader, progress.

adj. + prize

first, second, top, third, big, one, ultimate, great, major, special, main, richest, coveted, valuable, glittering, fabulous, fourth, grand, real, free, annual, fifth, literary, overall, individual, superb, official, international, small, super, equal, extra, political, supreme, single, exclusive, higher, monthly, wonderful, important, elusive, remarkable, maximum, attractive, new, reduced, added, brilliant, decent, additional, low, national, hard, enormous, excellent, full, pro, substantial, winner-takes-all, average, chief, original.

reward（n.）

❖ 例句

Mr. Joans offered a reward of NT$5,000 for information leading to the return of his missing dog.

Joans 先生提供五千元給任何提供消息使他找回他走失的狗的人作為賞金。

The intrinsic rewards of doing a "worthwhile" job may outweigh the glamour of wealth and success.

做一件自己認為有價值的工作所得到的回饋可能超過財富和成功的魅力。

❖ 常用搭配詞

the rewards of + n.

office, employment, reading, success.

adj. + reward

financial, high, rich, extrinsic, economic, just, those, greater, differential, potential, unequal, tangible, considerable, big, different, personal, real, determining, substantial, individual, material, possible, monetary, social, symbolic, same, valuable, adequate, specific, non-pecuniary, proper, further, indirect, new, occupational, contingent, long-term, suitable, extra, equitable, positive, political, offered, few, external, emotional, huge, occasional, intended, intrinsic, natural, intermittent.

bonus（n.）

❖ 例句

Each employee in this company receives a Christmas bonus.
這家公司的每一位員工都可以領聖誕節獎金。

❖ 常用搭配詞

n. + bonus

claim, Christmas, cash, early reply, strength, claims, no-claims, performance, loyalty, rank,（ten）percent, win, target, productivity, war, £10,000, tax, incentive, group, works, investment, hardship, share, democracy, pension.

bonus + n.

payments, scheme, points, system, shares, prize, issue, bonds, element, allocations, seal, rate, code, calculations, offer, target, surveyor, pay, money , marks, contract, strategy, section, tracks, period, screen, pool, structures, cheque, time.

adj. + bonus

added, special, unexpected, extra, real, additional, big, great, annual, terminal, welcome, tax-free, small, useful, final, earned, hidden, living, generous, two, large, further, new, free, nice, many, major, end-of-season, double, future, reversionary, electoral, valuable, profit-linked, guaranteed, possible, performance-related, financial, forward, handsome.

medal（n.）

❖ 例句

Desmond Doss was awarded a Bronze Star Medal for saving the lives of 75 wounded infantrymen in World War II.

Desmond Doss 因為在二次世界大戰中搭救75位受傷的步兵獲頒銅星勳章。

❖ 常用搭配詞

n. + medal

gold, bronze, silver, empire, gallantry, championship, cup,（Defence） Service, George, memorial, Edinburgh, memorial, campaign, war, Victoria, defence, Blue Water, jubilee, winners, police, team, anniversary, conduct, league, faraday, runners-up, place.

adj. + medal

gold, Olympic, monthly, three, commemorative, military, royal, silver, first, senior, contemporary, special, extra, genuine, polar, golden, winning, Italian, second, individual, silver- plated, long-service, prestigious, green, serious.

medal + n.

winner, ribbons, competition, hope, fight, prospect, success, position, triumph, chance, results, haul, time, ceremony, sale, award, podium.

trophy（n.）

❖ 例句

Apart from the trophy the winner receives NT$10,000.
除了獎盃以外優勝者還獲得台幣十萬元。

❖ 常用搭配詞

adj. + trophy

Regal, European, major, first, coveted, senior, indoor, Schneider, sporting, famous, second, prized, Prudential, national, magnificent, special, new, open, grisly, handsome, domestic, fine, personal, international, individual, great, annual, priceless, top, original.

n. + trophy

Natwest, Texaco, championship, memorial, west, year, challenge, autoglass, league, team, tennis, club, gold, crystal, autumn, world, silver, bowl, schools, challenger, star, stayers, sports, magazine, telegraph, golf, runners-up, Goodyear, tourist, champions, video, pairs, horse.

綜合整理

award	頒發某人做某件事情的獎品或獎金，前面常接獎項的名稱（如the Academy Award奧斯卡金像獎，Grammy Award葛萊美獎）。另外也指法律判賠的金額（如compensation award賠補償金）。
prize	頒給競賽優勝者的獎品或樂透等博弈獎金，前面常接獎項的名稱（如Nobel Prize諾貝爾獎，Pulitzer Prize普立茲獎）或獎金價值（如the £200,000 top prize價值二十萬頭獎）的名詞，或表示獎品等級（如first prize）或性質（valuable prize）的形容詞。
reward	努力工作或做好事得到的報酬回饋，前面常接有關酬勞性質、種類、及多少的形容詞，也會接酬勞金額（如£10,000 reward）。另外也指警方或個人的懸賞金。
bonus	正常薪資以外的獎金（如annual bonus年終獎金）。另外也指意外獲得的利益，以及保險公司的紅利。
medal	頒給競賽優勝者或有英勇事蹟者的錢幣大小圓形獎牌或勳章，通常繫有緞帶。前面常接獎項的名稱（如European Cup medal歐洲盃獎章）
trophy	頒給競賽優勝者的獎盃或盤狀獎牌。前面常接獎項的名稱。

補充：Bounty表示政府提供協助捉拿要犯等的懸賞金（如bounty hunter賞金獵人），在語料庫出現次數不高，因此未列入本項。Premium指額外津貼或商店為刺激購買的贈品，因為有多重意義，在此也未列入本項。

Unit 17 景象

StringNet語料庫出現次數

scene	sight	phenomenon	wonder	spectacle
8631	7002	3455	2255	1146

scene（n.）

❖ 例句

Her bedroom overlooks the coastal scene.
她的臥房俯瞰海岸的景色。

❖ 常用搭配詞

the scene of a + adj. + n.
   crime, accident, murder, crash, massacre.

n. + scene
   street, murder, battle, rave, death, railway, world, winter, country, city,
   garden, bedroom, party, Manchester, village, night, beach, crash, snow,
   landscape, mountain, harbor, common, attack, station.

adj. + scene
   this, international, political, whole, that, final, first, local, social, last,
   domestic, British, contemporary, gay, literary, particular, industrial,
   mad, passing, peaceful, underground, famous, familiar, racing,
   national, dramatic, similar, rural, educational, underwater, good,
   bad, terrible, pastoral, quiet, strange, climactic, unpleasant, entire,

current, great, beautiful, picturesque, idyllic, touching, urban, human, spectacular, cultural, nude, remarkable, natural, typical, extraordinary, actual, emotional, dreadful, impressive, cozy, colorful, ugly, charming, embarrassing, pleasant, tragic, bizarre, vibrant, coastal, appalling, awful, public, post-election, interesting, shocking, hilarious, unlikely.

sight（n.）

❖ 例句

Street artists are a common sight in Taipei.
在台北市街頭藝人很常見。
When he looked out the window, he saw a strange sight.
當他往窗外看，看到一個奇怪的景象。

❖ 常用搭配詞

adj. + sight

familiar, common, impressive, rare, strange, unusual, beautiful, awesome, sad, pitiful, spectacular, extraordinary, wonderful, amazing, pleasant, lovely, magnificent, terrible, splendid, bloody, remarkable, awe-inspiring, marvelous, pathetic, heartbreaking, bizarre, depressing, unforgettable, frequent, unexpected, dazzling, gruesome, astonishing, dreadful, unprecedented, nostalgic, charming, distressing.

adj. + sights

famous, spectacular, familiar, local, many, these, new, great, main, historic, common, fascinating, horrible, terrible, strange, wonderful, historical, beautiful, telescopic, remarkable, German, impressive, colorful, exotic, unusual, charming, fabulous, varied, amazing, welcome, splendid.

phenomenon（n.）

❖ 例句

The President issued a statement deploring the phenomenon of increasing domestic terrorism.

總統發表談話譴責國內恐怖主義增多的現象。

Given the advance of science, there are a lot of unexplained phenomena in the natural world.

縱然科學發達，自然界仍存有許多無法解釋的現象。

❖ 常用搭配詞

adj. + phenomenon

this, new, social, same, recent, common, general, natural, complex, rare, historical, modern, temporary, cultural, whole, strange, similar, universal, growing, interesting, urban, linguistic, remarkable, psychological, aesthetic, unusual, political, physical, dynamic, secondary, human, curious, literary, transient, mental, worldwide, local, familiar, worrying, national, inexplicable, unique, odd, widespread, striking, well-known, international , progressive, middle-class, self-cure, observed, alarming, cyclical, ongoing, geological, global, regional, biological, current, paradoxical.

the phenomenon of + n.

life, pornography, deixis, interference, identity, interest, shock.

wonder（n.）

❖ 例句

Snow is the wonder of the world.
雪是這世界的奇景。

❖ 常用搭配詞

adj. + wonder

natural, chinless, royal, real, scientific, architectural, modern, Swiss, one-season, scenic, perpetual, Portuguese, three-minute, one-time, constant, wide-eyed, absolute, strange, magical.

spectacle（n.）

❖ 例句

He tried not to make a spectacle with himself with an outburst of anger.
他試著不當眾暴怒以免出醜。

❖ 常用搭配詞

adj. + spectacle

public, magnificent, sporting, old, sad, dramatic, unique, great, bloody, awesome, ludicrous, thrilling, awful, patriotic, fascinating, odd, theatrical, pathetic, imaginary, extraordinary, embarrassing, expensive, extravagant, exhilarating, lovely, amazing, amusing, natural, grisly.

綜合整理

scene	親眼看到或在圖片中看到的地方風景（如street scene），也指戰爭、犯罪、或事故的現場（如battle scene）。另外有其他多種意義，最常用來指戲劇中的一場，也指某種活動的圈子（如art scene藝術圈）。
sight	泛指親眼看見的事物或景象，複數the sights表示觀光景點名勝。另外表示視覺、看見等多種意義。
phenomenon	存在或發生在較大範圍的現象，如國家社會（如global phenomenon全球性現象）、自然（如natural phenomenon自然現象）、或科學（如physical phenomenon物理現象）界等的現象，尤其是複雜難懂或少見的（如unexplained phenomenon無法解釋的現象）。另外也指少見的奇人。
wonder	令人驚異讚嘆的奇觀（如the Seven Wonders of the World世界七大奇觀）。
spectacle	1.精彩壯觀的景象（如magnificent spectacle壯麗的景觀）；2.親眼看到的不尋常或有趣的景象或事物，常有負面含意（如make a spectacle of oneself當眾出醜）。複數型spectacles表示眼鏡。

Unit 18 景色

StringNet語料庫出現次數

view	landscape	surroundings	scenery	vista
30685	3823	1230	749	250

view（n.）

❖ 例句

They booked a sea-view room in the hotel.

他們在這家飯店訂了一間有海景的房間。

He got a clear view of the firework from the top of the hotel.

他們在飯店的屋頂可以清楚看到煙火的景色。

❖ 常用搭配詞

adj. + view

such, panoramic, magnificent, spectacular, superb, fine, wonderful, splendid, breathtaking, lovely, beautiful, excellent, best, glorious, fantastic, fabulous, impressive, marvelous, picturesque, distant, coastal, lateral, scenic, clear, two-dimensional, surrouding, well-known, enchanting, stupendous, attractive, broad, aerial, perfect.

n. + view

sea, mountain, side, back, grandstand, park, perspective, hill, castle, church, west, garden, bay, lagoon, city, snapshot, closeup, tree.

landscape（n.）

❖ 例句

The garbage landfill is a blot on the landscape.
那座垃圾掩埋場破壞了附近的景觀。
There is a huge landscape painting on the wall of his office.
他的辦公室牆上掛著一幅很大的風景畫。

❖ 常用搭配詞

adj. + landscape

English, rural, urban, local, beautiful, British, familiar, natural, surrounding, historic, barren, wild, agricultural, rocky, ancient, whole, distant, rolling, wooded, striking, rugged, desolate, existing, alien, vast, French, high, wide, empty, undulating, Alpine, farmed, historical, spectacular, unique, snow-covered, southern, deserted, man-made, bare, attractive, frozen, treeless, hilly, wintry, fragile, extraordinary, Medieval, impressionist, amazing, craggy, sprawling, arable, scarred, created, mountainous.

landscape + n.

painting, design, architect, features, quality, change, gardener, painter, conservation, photographer, impact, drawings, types, pattern, protection, character, artists, historian, description, park, resources, framework, consultants, research, geometry, heritage, poetry, watercolors.

surroundings（n.）

❖ 例句

It's weird to see so many soldiers killing each other in the peaceful natural surroundings.
看一大群軍人在祥和的大自然環境中彼此殺戮感覺很詭異。

❖ 常用搭配詞

adj. +surroundings

new, beautiful, pleasant, familiar, rural, elegant, natural, comfortable, magnificent, peaceful, idyllic, strange, physical, picturesque, quiet, attractive, historic, exotic, lovely, spacious, salubrious, opulent, luxurious, primitive, sumptuous, tranquil, grand, domestic, breathtaking, aristocratic, spectacular, cultural, impressive, urban, wild.

scenery（n.）

❖ 例句

Few countries can rival Czechoslovakia for mountain scenery.
很少國家的山景可以和捷克的山景匹敵。

❖ 常用搭配詞

adj. + scenery

beautiful, spectacular, magnificent, dramatic, breathtaking, coastal, Alpine, stunning, passing, wonderful, surrounding, mountainous, varied, fantastic, best, superb, changing, delightful, exciting, glorious, finest, lovely, picturesque, remarkable, Austrian, attractive, placid, sensational, impressive, fascinating, contrasting, pleasant, sublime, splendid, English.

n. + scenery

mountain, cliff, limestone, valley, woodland, forest, river, rock.

vista（n.）

❖ 例句

From that position we could see the panorama vista of the river and field.
從那個位置我們可以看到河流和平原的全景。

❖ 常用搭配詞

adj. + vista

long, sweeping, beautiful, breathtaking, unexpected, panoramic, changing, impressive, broad.

綜合整理

view	從某處能夠看到某區域的範圍，尤其是風景，前面常接自然景觀名稱（如sea, mountain, lagoon）或是建築物名稱（如church, castle, city）。也指視線所及的範圍。另有其他意義，如看法、觀點。
landscape	鄉村自然景觀或風景畫，範圍較大，因此前面時常接國家或地區名稱（如Scottish landscape蘇格蘭風景），也表示人造景觀（如landscape design景觀設計）。另外也指某種地形（如rugged landscape 高低不平的地形）。
surroundings	在某個時間點某人或某物周遭的環境，包括自然景觀、建築物、或是物件等。
scenery	某國家或地區自然景觀特色，如山川、沙漠等，範圍較大。
vista	文學用字。從遠處看的風景，遠景。
補充：outlook表示從某處看出去的景色，但是此字的主要意義是對某事的態度看法，以及某件事情未來的前景，因此未列入本項。	

Unit 19 侵犯，干擾

StringNet語料庫出現次數

interference	interruption	infringement	trespass	encroachment
1421	545	449	244	205

interference（n.）

❖ 例句

In a press conference the President condemned foreign interference in our internal affairs.

總統在一場記者會中譴責外國干涉我國內政事務。

❖ 常用搭配詞

adj. + interference

political, outside, adverse, human, foreign, unlawful, unwarranted, concurent, external, gross, possible, differential, alleged, electrical, wrongful, bureaucratic, physical, unreasonable, proactive, mutual, undue, government, direct, papal, serious, unacceptable, proprietorial,, intolerable, flagrant, supernatural, ministerial, judicial, minimum, constant, intentional, soviet, unconstitutional, unjustified, blatant, well-meant, perceived, surgical, increasing, minimal, constructive, military, experimental, illegal, official, unwelcome, overt, required.

v. + interference

prevent, avoid, tolerate, have, state, direct, suffer, cause, justify.

interruption（n.）

❖ 例句

It is hard to finish your talk in the debate without interruption.
在辯論會中你很難在發言時不被打斷。

❖ 常用搭配詞

 adj. + interruption

　constant, temporary, further, major, brief, unplanned, these, many, few, more, fewer, repeated, endless, surgical, perpetual, unnecessary, momentary, consequent, mere, minor, unwelcome, several, rude, short.

 verb. + interruption

　accept, get, avoid, constitute.

infringement（n.）

❖ 例句

The writer filed a copyright infringement suit against the publisher.
這位作家對這家出版社提出侵犯版權的訴訟。

❖ 常用搭配詞

 adj. + infringement

　any, alleged, minor, repeated, possible, secondary, serious, further, clear, technical, marginal, definite, unjustifiable, unacceptable, persistent, original.

n. + infringement

copyright, patent, mark, trademark.

trespass（n.）

❖ 例句

The fan took an aerial photograph of the movie star's house and was sued for trespass to land.

那位粉絲拍了那位電影明星住家的空拍照而因此被告非法闖入私人土地。

❖ 常用搭配詞

adj. + trespass

mass, criminal, unintentional, continuing, great, intentional.

v. + a trespass

constitute, commit.

encroachment（n.）

❖ 例句

Wildlife in this area is dwindling because of the encroachment of agricultural people on the land.

此地區的野生動植物因為農地逐漸侵占土地而數量愈來愈少。

❖ 常用搭配詞

adj. + encroachment

urban, gradual, direct, further, steady, serious, communist, Japanese, royal, massive.

n. + encroachment

government, sand, desert.

綜合整理

interference	未經同意干涉某件事情。前面時常是政治、軍事、法律、政府、或國家等的形容詞（如political interference政治干涉、American interference美國干涉）。
interruption	干擾別人談話或某件事情的進行。可數名詞。
infringement	侵犯別人法律上的權利。前面常接版權、專利、商標等名詞（如patent infringement侵犯專利）。
trespass	未經同意進入私人土地。
encroachment	逐漸侵占愈來愈多別人的土地、時間、財產、以及權利。前面很少接及物動詞，大多是動詞 + 介系詞（如lead to, control against, whine about）

Unit 20 傾向，性情

StringNet語料庫出現次數

tendency	disposition	inclination	temperament	propensity	leaning
3583	846	652	621	338	106

tendency（n.）

❖ 例句

This study indicates that criminal tendencies may be inherited.
這個研究指出犯罪傾向有可能是來自遺傳。

There is a tendency for most companies to be inward-looking.
大部分的公司都傾向只顧自己。

❖ 常用搭配詞

adj. + tendency

this, natural, general, increasing, strong, growing, greater, marked, common, clear, suicidal, inherent, aggressive, similar, increased, slight, central, underlying, innate, contradictory, dominant, criminal, dangerous, political, homosexual, violent, centrifugal, inbuilt, unfortunate, anti-social, human, universal, persistent, inflationary, opposite, traditional, artistic, certain, bleeding, consistent, significant, genetic, pronounced, conservative, psychological, negative, addictive, subversive, inherited, habitual, evil, behavioral, cultural, prevailing, feminine, moral.

a tendency to + Vroot

regard, become, treat, look, think, use, make, assume, deprave, fall, have, give, view, do, accept, say, interpret, reduce, blame, allow, change, focus, overdo, wander, build, equate, concentrate, report, exaggerate, produce, impose, identify, forget, repeat, move, try.

disposition（n.）

❖ 例句

She was of a nervous disposition.
她很容易緊張。
Many women have a disposition toward obedience.
很多女性個性傾向服從。

❖ 常用搭配詞

adj. + disposition

nervous, sunny, liberal, cheerful, friendly, criminal, pleasant, peaceful, jealous, aggressive, conservative, placid, cynical, strong, political, happy.

inclination（n.）

❖ 例句

She showed no inclination to argue with him.
她看起來一點也不想和他爭辯。
His natural inclination was to dodge the coming ball.
他的本能是躲開飛來的球。

❖ 常用搭配詞

adj. + inclination

natural, little, personal, spontaneous, slightest, axial, low, merest, political, much, greater, powerful, first, reduced.

inclination to + Vroot

do, go, take, become, join, leave, look, find, use, learn, act, record, pursue, think, help, experiment, practice, get, write, start, avoid, spend, reject, treat, run.

temperament（n.）

❖ 例句

He was of an anxious and dependent temperament , especially when faced with pressure.
他天性很容易焦慮和依賴別人，尤其是面臨壓力時。

❖ 常用搭配詞

adj. + temperament

artistic, good, excellent, different, particular, scientific, equable, nervous, passionate, volatile, psychotic, uncertain, sanguine, saturnine, mercurial, fragile, phlegmatic, lovely, questionable, romantic, ideal, strange, morbid.

propensity （n.）

❖ 例句

There are always potential risks of transplant surgery due to the propensity of the body's defences to reject foreign tissue.
移植手術始終存有風險，因為人體的防禦機制會本能地排斥外來的組織。

❖ 常用搭配詞

adj. + propensity

　marginal, high, average, increased, behavior, different, natural, moral.

propensity to + Vroot

　consume, save, import, move, take, break, report, marry, innovate, produce, strike, engage.

leaning （n.）

❖ 例句

In high school he displayed a leaning towards the stage.
在中學時代他迷上舞台表演。

❖ 常用搭配詞

adj. + leaning

　political, ideological, homosexual, socialist, religious, feminist, literary, fascist.

綜合整理

tendency	人天生的行為傾向（如natural tendency自然的傾向, inherent tendency天生的傾向），或事物的改變傾向。後面常接不定詞（for + N）to do something或介系詞to/toward/for + N。
disposition	正式用字，個人思想意念或性情的特質使得他容易做出某種行為或有某種反應。和temperament相似。後面可以接不定詞to do something或介系詞toward/of + N。另外有配置、處理決定、轉讓等多種其他意義。
inclination	一般想做某件事情的傾向（如natural inclination自然的傾向），或特定思想或行為的傾向。後面可以接不定詞to do something，常用在否定片語show no inclination to do something，也可接介系詞toward/of + N。
temperament	個人整體個性的喜怒哀樂等情緒的傾向。在語料庫前面最常出現的形容是artistic, artistic temperament是醫學名詞，用來形容作家、藝術家、和音樂作曲共有的性情，嚴重時會出現憂鬱、極端等精神失調。而artistic tendency可能指個人的藝術性向、外在的藝術潮流、也可指具有藝術家的性格。此字可用在以星座或中世紀生理學中所謂的四種體液所構成的個性傾向。
propensity	正式用字，人類天性使然的行為舉止傾向。後面可以接不定詞to do something。
leaning	喜好的傾向，後面常接介系詞toward。

Unit 21 傾斜

StringNet語料庫出現次數

lean	slope	tip	tilt	slant
4476	2337	1653	721	179

lean（vi.）

❖ 例句

She leaned forward and kissed his cheek.

她的身體向前傾斜去親吻他的臉頰。

Do not lean back on the chair.

不要向後靠在椅子上。

❖ 常用搭配詞

lean + adv.

　forward, closer, across, forwards, heavily, away, backwards, more, right, slightly, weakly, together, hard, sideways, further, outwards, casually, inwards, earnestly, easily, quickly, gently, outside, confidentially, lazily, nervously, wearily, drunkenly, slowly, sharply, cautiously, lightly, unsteadily.

lean + prep.

　against, on, over, towards, across, into, in, to, at, from, toward, upon.

slope（vi.）

❖ 例句

The lawn slopes down to the river.
那片草地斜向河邊。

❖ 常用搭配詞

slope + adv.

   down, off, up, gently, downwards, away, steeply, slightly, upwards, back, inwards, downhill, more, quite, downward.

slope + prep.

   to, towards, from, like, for, at, in, with.

n. (s) + slope

   ground, garden, ceiling, lawn, sides, bank, land, road, buildings, hill, floor, grass.

tip（vi./vt.）

❖ 例句

Don't tip your chair on its rear legs.
不要把你的椅子往後翹起。
This year world population tipped the scales at five billion.
今年全球人口高達五十億人。

❖ 常用搭配詞

tip the + _n._

　　scales, balance, chair, mirror, scale, table, boat, glass, bottle.

_n. (s)_ + tip

　　head, man, chair, boy, glass, hat, hair, scales, top, lorry, hadn, tendency, pears, truck.

tilt（vi./vt.）

❖ 例句

He was sleeping with his head tilting to one side.
他在睡覺，頭歪到一邊。

❖ 常用搭配詞

_n. (s)_ + tilt

　　head, chin, face, floor, mouth, chair, world, hat, body, wings, cliffs, lipts, hand, room, balance, plane.

tilt + _adv._

　　back, slightly, up, forward, away, upwards, backwards, over, downwards, down, forwards, horizontally, defiantly, sharply.

tilt the + _n._

　　balance, head, bottle, lens, card.

slant（vi./vt.）

❖ 例句

The sun slanted through the window, shadowing her face.
陽光從窗戶斜射進來，在她的臉產生陰影。
Her eyes slanted in her mother's direction.
她的目光斜向她母親的方向。
He slanted her a quick look.
他很快地斜眼看她一下。

❖ 常用搭配詞

n.（s）+ slant
  sun, eyes, light, sunlight, glance, gaze, sunshine, moonlight.

slant + adv.
  in, down, up, over, away.

綜合整理

lean	不及物動詞，後面一定要接介系詞或副詞。表示人的身體向某個方向傾斜，或物品斜靠在某處，語料庫中的句子主詞大多是人。
slope	不及物動詞，地面或平面傾斜。主詞通常是建築物或地面相關名詞。
tip	及物或不及物動詞。表示傾斜或使傾斜，常用在片語tip the scales/balance表示扭轉局勢，造成改變。和tilt相似。此字可當名詞和動詞，意義眾多，當動詞時另外也表示打翻、顛覆等意義。
tilt	及物或不及物動詞。表示傾斜或使傾斜，尤其是人體頭部或四肢局部的傾斜。當名詞時可表示偏見。
slant	及物或不及物動詞。表示傾斜或使傾斜，主詞時常是光線（如sunlight, moonlight）或眼神。另外也表示人的意見傾向某一方面。當名詞時可表示偏見或斜線。

Unit 22 缺點

StringNet語料庫出現次數

disadvantage	defect	drawback	flaw	shortcoming	downside
2000	1504	584	520	483	90

disadvantage（n.）

❖ 例句

There are advantages and disadvantages to either.

這二者各有優缺點。

❖ 常用搭配詞

the advantage of + n.

others, women, uncertainty, devolution, deformation, monarchy, market-orientation, over-exposure.

v. + disadvantage

has, have, had, avoid, suffer, lessen.

adj. + disadvantage

main, social, major, one, economic, only, obvious, competitive, serious, great, sever, racial, considerable, distinct, possible, ethnic, real, educational, potential, slight, long-term, additional, many, environmental, unfair, locational, commercial, psychological, political, multiple, electoral, perceived, inherent, strategic, specific, definite, tactical, practical, tremendous, corresponding, permanent.

defect（n.）

❖ 例句

Dioxin can cause liver damage, miscarriage, birth defects, and cancer.
戴奧辛可能造成肝臟損壞、流產、新生兒缺陷、以及癌症。

❖ 常用搭配詞

adj. + defect

congenital, serious, latent, genetic, structural, major, physical, minor, visual, inherent, mechanical, zero, procedural, specific, basic, hidden, developmental, mental, principal, jurisdictional, primary, alleged, great, substantial, fundamental, immune, inherited, technical, underlying, main, obvious, certain, organizational, septal, formal, immunological, chief, relevant, behavioral, perceived, glaring, cognitive, manifest, common, metabolic, related, slight, residual, regulatory, initial, electrical.

n. + defect

birth, neural tube, building, sight, eye, heart, design, character, speech, enzyme, housing, quality, transport, vehicle, gene, vision.

v. + the defect

remedy, has, discovered.

drawback（n.）

❖ 例句

The main drawback of living in the country for him is solitude.
對他而言住在鄉間最大的缺點是孤單。

❖ 常用搭配詞

adj. + drawback

one, major, only, main, serious, another, potential, big, real, slight, obvious, second, possible, considerable, greatest, principal, apparent, great, chief.

flaw（n.）

❖ 例句

He felt that there was some flaw in her argument but was unable to pinpoint it precisely.
他覺得她的論點有瑕疵但卻無法準確地指出。

❖ 常用搭配詞

adj. + flaw

fatal, fundamental, one, major, serious, basic, main, cosmetic, second, crucial, conceptual, real, single.

flaw in the + n.

use, system, voters, idea.

shortcoming（n.）

❖ 例句

He is writing a book on the shortcomings of the existing local government system.

他在寫一本關於現行地方政府制度缺點的書。

❖ 常用搭配詞

adj. + shortcoming

　this, one, some, another, serious, much-discussed.

downside（n.）

❖ 例句

The downside of being rich is that you never know who your true friends are.

有錢的缺點就是你無法知道誰是你真實的朋友。

❖ 常用搭配詞

adj. + downside

　limited, devastating.

綜合整理

disadvantage	造成某個人或某件事情成功或有果效的機會降低的問題或不利條件。常用在片語advantages and disadvantages表示權衡事情的利弊。片語the disadvantage of + N 當中的名詞N可能是造成問題的對象（如the disadvantage of women）或問題本身（如the disadvantage of deformation）。也用來表示弱勢（如ethnic disadvantage 種族弱勢）。
defect	造成某個人或某件事情不完美的缺陷，如錯誤或缺失。前面時常接形容詞或名詞表示人體的缺陷（如immune defect免疫系統缺陷，heart defect心臟缺陷）。
drawback	某種情況、計畫、或產品的不利條件或缺點等。前面常接major或main來分析某個情況的主要缺點。
flaw	造成某件事情不完美的錯誤、瑕疵、或弱點。和defect相似，但是程度可能較嚴重，常用在片語fatal flaw表示致命的錯誤。
shortcoming	造成某個人或某件事情成功或有效的機會降低的錯誤或弱點。
downside	某種情況的負面因素。在語料庫資料不多。

Unit 23 證實，證明，確認

StringNet語料庫出現次數

prove	confirm	affirm	verify	validate	substantiate	corroborate
14571	8525	633	570	470	311	102

prove（vt.）

❖ 常用句型

> S + prove + O + adj.
> S + prove + that + 子句

❖ 例句

I can prove them all wrong.

我可以證明他們全都錯了。

Can you prove that he is the murderer？

你可以證明他就是殺人兇手嗎？

❖ 常用搭配詞

prove + adj.

difficult, useful, impossible, successful, right, wrong, popular, invaluable, possible, effective, fatal, inadequate, necessary, correct, attractive, crucial, expensive, irresistible, disastrous, elusive, unable, decisive, valuable, unfounded, insufficient, costly, helpful, negative, acceptable, incapable, fruitless, disappointing, easy, satisfactory, beneficial, short-lived, defective, unsuitable, dangerous, positive, groundless, controversial, embarrassing, troublesome, good, profitable, true, unwilling, impractical, justified, abortive, guilty, vital, illusory, inconclusive, significant, intractable, innocent, accurate, problematic, interesting, adept, reliable, unworkable, indispensable, feasible, permanent, convenient, viable.

confirm（vt.）

❖ 常用句型

S + confirm + O
S + confirm + that + 子句

❖ 例句

He wrote to confirm the reservation he made on the phone on Friday 13th Sep.
他寫信去確認他在九月十三日星期五打電話去的訂房。
This photo confirmed my suspicion.
這張照片證實我的懷疑。

❖ 常用搭配詞

confirm the + n.

presence, existence, view, importance, diagnosis, fact, impression, appointment, booking, validity, trend, report, opinion, order, idea, need, accuracy, price, letter, result, decision, company, extent, position, belief, claim, name, authenticity, increase, pattern, reduction, superiority, choice, use, figure, sense, dominance, absence, theory, route, correctness, number, story, strength, finding, plan, notion, progress, point, commission, efficacy, assignment, identity, right, involvement, adequacy, type, conclusion, picture, information, recovery, date, purchase, suspicion, truth, possibility, conversation.

affirm（vt.）

❖ 常用句型

S + affirm + O
S + affirm + that + 子句

❖ 例句

That rumor has never been affirmed.
那個謠言從來沒有被證實過。
The President affirmed that he had divorced his wife.
總統公開聲明他已經和他的妻子離婚。

❖ 常用搭配詞

affirm the + n.

right, decision, need, importance, value, contract, call, presence, commitment, worth, principle, agreement, possibility, judge.

verify（vt.）

❖ 常用句型

> **S + verify + O**
> **S + verify + that + 子句**

❖ 例句

The judge ordered an official investigation to verify the authenticity of the will.
法官下令正式調查來證實此遺囑是否是真的。

❖ 常用搭配詞

verify the + _n._
　accuracy, information, petition, authenticity, identity, fact.

validate（vt.）

❖ 常用句型

> **S+ validate + O**

❖ 例句

You need to apply for a certificate to validate your test results.
你必須申請一份證書來證實你的考試結果。

All the information used in the paper has been validated.
這篇報告中的資訊都經過證實。

❖ 常用搭配詞

validate the + n.

concept, consent, atrocity, disks, view, occurrence, effectiveness.

substantiate（vt.）

❖ 常用句型

S + substantiate + O

❖ 例句

There is no evidence to substantiate his claim.
沒有證據可以證明他的說詞。

❖ 常用搭配詞

substantiate the + n.

claim, detail, authenticity, gossip.

corroborate（vt.）

❖ 常用句型

S + corroborate + O

❖ 例句

The new evidence corroborated the prosecutor's hypothesis.

新的證物證實了檢察官的假設。

❖ 常用搭配詞

corroborate the + n.

　report, theory, allegation, testimony, finding.

綜合整理

confirm	確定某件事情的真實性，可能藉著證據，也表示確定某個安排事件的有效性。時常用在不定詞以表示目的（如to write to confirm...）。常用於被動語態。
affirm	正式用字。公開聲明某件事情的真實性，或加強某個信念的強度。
verify	正式用字。確定某件事情的真實性或正確性，可能藉著證據。也是法律用語，表示作證。常用於被動語態。
validate	正式用字，確定某件事情的真實性、正確性、或合法性，可能藉著正式或有法律效力的文件。另外也表示使生效。和confirm相似。常用於被動語態。
substantiate	正式用字，證明某人所說的話是真的。
corroborate	藉著證據確定或加強某人的言論的真實性。和confirm相似，但是受詞時常是言論。

Unit 24 權力

StringNet語料庫出現次數

power	authority	jurisdiction	sovereignty	dominion
38096	31048	2115	1208	409

power（n.）

❖ 例句

He came to power in 1986 after a South African-backed coup.
他在1986年一場由非洲支持的政變後取得政權。

❖ 常用搭配詞

the + _n._ of power

balance, exercise, distribution, transfer, concentration, concept, reins, abuse, center, structure, levers, devolution, possession, division, centralization, pursuit, sense, hierarchy, feeling, seat, assumption, shift, basis, reality, relations, definition, influence, game, legitimacy, ministry, violence, experience, ring, heart, polarization, notion.

adj. + power

legislative, political, economic, national, real, full, western, European, considerable, legal, military, colonial, presidential, foreign, royal, imperial, personal, central, absolute, social, internal, sovereign, healing, magical, Soviet, judicial, public, enormous, dark, black, governmental, delegated, bureaucratic, allied, spiritual, supernatural, executive, divine, administrative, mystical, physical, mental, arbitrary, constitutional, ultimate, compulsory, American, supreme, regional, communist, human, unequal, dominant, evil, dynamic, white, cultural, usurped, regulatory, legitimate, rival, federal, rising, domestic, democratic, third, catholic, parliamentary, law-making, natural, autocratic, governing, patriarchal, declining.

authority（n.）

❖ 例句

The protesters wanted to see someone in authority.
抗議人士要見有職權的人。

❖ 常用搭配詞

authority to + v.

make, have, forgive, allot, provide, receive, impose, control, investigate, refuse, raise, issue, use, keep, accept, minimize, initiate, determine, award, resist, pass, incur, establish, remove, exert, order, seek, improve.

adj. + authority

public, political, regulatory, Soviet, legislative, unitary, legal, statutory, royal, leading, relevant, national, legitimate, French, lawful, judicial, constitutional, federal, Israeli, Chinese, ultimate, full, delegated, administrative, appointing, international, personal, governmental, parental, municipal, supervisory, supreme, regulating, established, overall, imperial, elected, charismatic, cultural, colonial, communist, absolute, controlling, parliamentary, effective, white, responsible, presidential, governing, administering, catholic.

jurisdiction （n.）

❖ 例句

The Supreme Court has jurisdiction over the state courts.

最高法院對州法院有管轄權。

❖ 常用搭配詞

jurisdiction to + n.

make, hear, determine, decide, review, grant, confer, entertain, order, consider, deal, do, investigate, wind, try, punish, set, attach, award, stand, cover, override, rectify, authorize, allow, supervise, strike.

adj. + jurisdiction

inherent, exclusive, civil, appellate, supervisory, competent, criminal, territorial, limited, compulsory, original, papal, visitorial, full, wide, concurrent, disciplinary, secular, spiritual, national, foreign, local, Russian, equitable, domestic, superior, discretionary, republican, legal, British, personal, military, supreme, relevant, human, royal, administrative, advisory, direct, subordinate, unrestricted.

sovereignty（n.）

❖ 例句

In April 1832, Britain proclaimed sovereignty over the Falkland Isles.
在1832年英國公開宣佈擁有福克蘭群島的主權。

❖ 常用搭配詞

the sovereignty of (the) + n.

  parliament, people, nation, state, God, government, commons, consumer.

v. + the sovereignty

  proclaim, restore, maintain, recognize, reject, extend, limit, preserve.

dominion（n.）

❖ 例句

Some people believe that humans have been given the right to have dominion over animals.
有些人認為人類被賦予管理動物的權利。

❖ 常用搭配詞

dominion of（the）+ n.

  Canada, New England, Habsburgs, world, king-duke.

dominion over + n.

  nature, animals.

綜合整理

power	掌控或影響的能力，如政權、警察公權力。另外也指電力。
authority	機構或職位的職權。較常指政府當局或相關單位。
jurisdiction	法律上的司法審判權或管轄權。
sovereignty	國家的主權，統治權。
dominion	統治權、支配權。另外也表示領土。

Unit 25 全套裝備

StringNet語料庫出現次數

kit	outfit
2219	1094

kit（n.）

❖ 例句

She always brings her make-up kit with her.
她總是隨身攜帶她的化妝盒。
What should be included in the first aid kit?
急救箱裡面應該包含哪些東西?

❖ 常用搭配詞

n. + kit

　drum, press, software development, first aid, conversion, construction, tool, media, survival, car, aircraft, repair, armor, emergency, make-up, cleaning, garage, computer, bike repair, shaving, soccer, football, sports.

outfit（n.）

❖ 例句

Where have I seen the cowboy outfit before?

我以前好像在哪裡看過這套牛仔裝。

The boy wore a ninja outfit to the costume party.

這位男孩穿著忍者裝去參加化裝舞會。

❖ 常用搭配詞

n. + outfit

heavy metal, leather, punk, cowboy, stage, ninja, film, dance, racing, wedding, superhero, hip-hop, maid, tire repair, drum and bass, ski.

綜合整理

kit	針對某目的或是活動所使用的裝備（例如first aid kit, drum kit）。另外也可以表示電子設備，尤其是電腦方面。也可以指軍人或水手等的裝備。
outfit	包含配件的整套服裝，尤其是特殊場合的服裝（例如punk outfit, racing outfit）。
在英式英文中這二個字的意思互換，也就是kit表示某種目的使用的服裝（例如sports kit, football kits），而outfit則是全套工具（例如tire repair outfit）。	

Unit 26 希望

StringNet語料庫出現次數

hope	wish
8417	2926

hope（vi./vt./n.）

❖ 常用句型

> **S + hope +（that）子句**

❖ 例句

I hope everything in your new coffee shop goes well.
我希望你的新咖啡館一切順利。
She has given up all hope of having children.
她已經放棄生孩子的希望。

❖ 常用搭配詞

adj. +hope

high, great, false, own, many, best, faint, early, British, main, Olympic, pious, lingering, labor, vain, few, unfulfilled, liberal, dashed, personal, remaining, real, last, white, wild, bright, renewed, disappointed, lost, economic, inflated, political, fading, different, fresh, human, young, good, foolish, current, frustrated, public, blighted, initial, cherished, extravagant, growing, grand.

v. + hopes of

    have, raise, abandon, entertain, end, wreck cherish, offer, dash.

wish（vt./n.）

❖ 常用句型

> **S + wish +（that）子句**

❖ 例句

I wish I were a bird.
我希望我是一隻小鳥。
Close your eyes and make three wishes.
眼睛閉上許三個願望。

❖ 常用搭配詞

adj. + wish

    best, good, own, parental, expressed, last, personal, three, local, individual, human, warm, German, secret, insured, known, true, special, forbidden, real, murderous, get-well, American, ascertainable, sincere, original.

v. + a wish

    express, make, have, imply.

綜合整理

hope	希望某件事情發生或成真，而且相信此事是有可能發生的。當名詞時表示盼望。
wish	希望某件事情發生或成真，即使知道此事不可能發生。也表示祝福，希望某人發生好事。當名詞表示願望。

Unit 27 下降，下沉

StringNet語料庫出現次數

sink	descend	plunge	dive	plummet
3030	1666	1366	1048	78

sink（vi.）

❖ 常用句型

> **S + sink**

❖ 例句

His heart sank when he heard the bad news.
當他聽到那個壞消息，他的心情整個下沉。
If animals or men go into the quick sand, they will sink into it and die.
如果動物或人類走入流沙，他們會沉下去而滅頂。

❖ 常用搭配詞

n.（s）＋ sink

heart, words, head, spirits, voice, feet, boat sun, teeth, ships, fingers, body, shaft, water, hand, dog, kitchen, meaning, Maggie（人名）, titanic, chin, man, order, eyes, stomach, achievement, aircraft, submarine, money, sand, cross, rates, eggs, bait, wheels, vessel, heels.

descend（vi./vt.）

❖ 常用句型

> **S + descend（+O）**

❖ 例句

He descended the staircase into the basement.
他下樓梯到地下室。
The path descended into a valley after we walked for about one hour.
我們走了約一小時後，前面的路下坡到一個山谷。

❖ 常用搭配詞

n.（s）+ descend

silence, path, mouth, peace, spirit, fog, road, hush, men, gloom, hand, darkness, clam, curtain, people, stream, ladder, footsteps, ridge, track, god, water, misery, staircase, route, mist, fear, way, slopes, summit.

descend the + n.

stairs, steps, ladder, mountain, staircase, hillside, escalator, station, stone.

plunge（vi.）

❖ 常用句型

S + plunge（to + N）

❖ 例句

Her family was plunged into grief after her father died in an accident.
她的父親在一場意外中喪生後她的全家陷入悲痛之中。
The helicopter was hit and plunged into the sea.
那架直升機被擊中後落入海中。

❖ 常用搭配詞

n.（s）+ plunge

shares, profits, prices, car, index, horse, sales, pound, helicopter, ship, train, hands, focus, night, weight, fingers, water, cliffs, heart, floor, economy.

dive（vi.）

❖ 常用句型

S + dive（into +N）

❖ 例句

The glider dived almost vertically.

那架滑翔機幾乎是垂直墜落。

The pound dived to a record low of 2.438 against the German mark.

英鎊對馬克的比價降到2.438的新低。

❖ 常用搭配詞

n.（s） + dive

men, profits, soldiers, swallows, crust, shares, plane.

plummet（vi.）

❖ 常用句型

> **S + plummet（to +N）**
> **S + plummet from + N to + N**

❖ 例句

The hawk plummeted - dead from dehydration.

那隻隼因為脫水而從空中筆直落下死亡。

❖ 常用搭配詞

n.（s） + plummet

profits, prices, eagle.

綜合整理

sink	及物或不及物動詞。下沉到液體表面以下，或降低高度，也可以指心情下沉。
descend	及物或不及物動詞。正式用字。降低高度、斜下、身體往下。在文學上也指黑暗或某種感覺降臨。另外descend from表示是 ... 的後裔。
plunge	及物或不及物動詞。突然落下，價格或速率大幅下降。另外也指突然快速移動，或突然陷入某種狀況。語料庫常出現被動be plunged into表示突然陷入某種狀況，尤其是負面狀況。
dive	不及物動詞。原本表示潛水，也指在空中下降或在水中下沉，或數字或價格突然大幅下降。另外也指突然快速移動（如dive for cover尋找掩護）。
plummet	不及物動詞。從高處突然落下，也指價值或數量大幅下降。和plunge相似。

Unit 28 消失

StringNet語料庫出現次數

disappear	vanish
5305	1511

disappear（vi.）

❖ 常用句型

> **S + disappear（+ prep. +N）**

❖ 例句

He said goodbye to her and disappeared into the dark street.
他和她道別後就消失在漆黑的街道。
The boat sailed toward the horizon and eventually disappeared from sight.
船朝向地平線航行，最後消失在眼簾中。

❖ 常用搭配詞

<u>adv.</u> + disappear

just, virtually, simply, completely, suddenly, largely, gradually, finally, mysteriously, entirely, quickly, rapidly, eventually, totally, slowly, actually, apparently, quietly, nearly, really, practically, immediately, temporarily, literally, promptly, abruptly, mostly, shortly, politely, inevitably, consequently, miraculously, subsequently.

vanish（vi.）

❖ 常用句型

> **S + vanish（+ prep. +N）**

❖ 例句

The magician made the rabbit vanish into the air.
魔術師把兔子憑空消失。
His good mood vanished with the sudden rain.
他的好心情因為這場突如其來的雨而頓時消失。

❖ 常用搭配詞

 n.（s） + vanish

smile, connections, lady, look, scene, impression, bike, woman, shadow, grin, appetite, ability, sun, emotions, childhood, image, illness, planes, fear, depression.

 adv. + vanish

mysteriously, simply, virtually, suddenly, soon, completely, totally, quickly, promptly, finally, immediately, entirely, instantly, eventually, abruptly.

綜合整理

disappear	消失不見，無法用眼睛看到。
vanish	突然消失不見或不復存在，尤其是因為神祕不可知的原因。語料庫的句子常表示某個表情或情緒突然消失。

Unit 29 消除，消滅

StringNet語料庫出現次數

remove	eliminate	eradicate	extinguish	annihilate
11286	2406	457	320	139

remove（vt.）

❖ 常用句型

> **S + remove + O（+ from + N）**

❖ 例句

Do you have some cleaner that will remove ink stains?
你有可以去除墨水污漬的清潔劑嗎?

❖ 常用搭配詞

remove the + _n._

  need, child, paper, right, possibility, children, risk, power, danger, cause, threat, problem, incentive, uncertainty, anomaly, barrier, necessity, distinction, obstacles, causes, fear, effect, opportunity, obstruction, requirement, restriction, pollutants, bottleneck, debris, relics.

adv. + remove

  easily, entirely, completely, effectively, forcibly, surgically, totally, finally, quickly, eventually, successfully, largely, physically, progressively, subsequently, gradually, probably, slightly, suddenly, rapidly, immediately, simply, permanently, partly, safely, gently, painlessly, accidently, hastily, selectively, mysteriously, virtually, inadvertently.

eliminate（vt.）

❖ 常用句型

> **S + eliminate + O**

❖ 例句

There are several measures that can be taken to reduce or eliminate the problem.
有幾個方法可以減輕或除去這個問題。

❖ 常用搭配詞

eliminate + n.

 waste, competition, poverty, problems, people, discrimination, uncertainty, weaknesses, sexism, corruption, tariffs, conflicts, hazards, subsidies, duplication, risk, apartheid, errors, lead, barriers, differences, fraud, toxins, flooding, losses, tax, reliance, conflict, dust, obstacles, competitors.

eliminate the + n.

 need, possibility, risk, problem, use, deficit, ability, virus, danger, chance, surplus, organism, source, difference, minority, uncertainty, waste, influence, infection, duplication.

adv. + remove

completely, largely, entirely, totally, eventually, effectively, simply, progressively, gradually, necessarily, finally, systematically, supposedly, actually, immediately, probably, merely, quickly, practically, ruthlessly.

eradicate（vt.）

❖ 常用句型

S + eradicate + O

❖ 例句

The disease has been completely eradicated from this country.
在這個國家這個疾病已經被澈底消除了。

❖ 常用搭配詞

adv. + eradicate

completely, successfully, entirely, totally, gradually, wholly.

eradicate + n.

malaria, poverty, drug, tumors, group, Christianity, terrorism, anxiety, illiteracy, violence, inflation, helicobacter.

n. + to eradicate

attempt, effort, need, choice, desire, duty, campaign, treatment, way, failure.

extinguish（vt.）

❖ 常用句型

> **S + extinguish +O**

❖ 例句

After two hours the fire was finally extinguished.
過了二個鐘頭火勢終於被撲滅了。

❖ 常用搭配詞

adv. + extinguish

quickly, finally, completely, abruptly, eventually, nearly, totally.

n. + be extinguished

fires, sun light, lights.

extinguish the + n.

fire, flames, blaze, remainder, light.

annihilate（vt.）

❖ 常用句型

> **S + annihilate +O**

❖ 例句

After a bloody battle the government army annihilated the guerrillas.
經過一場血腥的戰鬥後政府軍消滅了游擊隊員。

❖ 常用搭配詞

annihilate the + n.
  ego, bowlers, elite, opponent.

n. + be annihilated
  army, bodies, forces, Jerusalem.

adv. + annihilate
  totally, immediately, virtually, largely.

綜合整理

remove	除去某個東西使它不復存在，受詞通常是無生命的物質。在字典中最主要的意義是移走，移去。
eliminate	除去不需要或是不想要的東西，相當於口語的get rid of。也表示消滅敵人，在比賽中則常用被動表示被淘汰出局。
eradicate	徹底消除某個不好或認為不好的東西，後面時常接有負面意義的名詞，如疾病、問題、或認為不好的思想價值。
extinguish	消除某個想法或感覺。較常表示滅火。
annihilate	徹底消滅某事物或人，受詞可以是人事物。在比賽中則是指輕易擊敗某人或某隊。

Unit 30 羞辱

StringNet語料庫出現次數

shame	insult	humiliation	disgrace	stigma
1834	698	616	478	278

shame（n.）

❖ 例句

There is no shame in admitting that you don't understand something you have read.
承認你看不懂你所讀過的東西並不可恥。
He bowed his head in shame.
他羞愧地低下頭。

❖ 常用搭配詞

v. + in shame
　bow, cry, blush.

adj. + shame
　great, crying, real, awful, secret, wicked, eternal, damned.

insult（n.）

❖ 例句

The manager had the employee stand and hurled insults at him for one hour.

經理要那位員工站著然後辱罵他一小時。

He won't tolerate the public insult and will retaliate.

他不會容忍這公開的羞辱，一定會反擊的。

❖ 常用搭配詞

<u>adj.</u> + insult

personal, final, ultimate, deliberate, verbal, gross, added, calculated, profound, direct, terrible, gratuitous, implied, subtle, racial, crude, public, genotoxic, bloody, racist, affectionate, ritual, stinging, absolute, disgraceful.

<u>v.</u> + insults

shout, hurl, exchange, mouth, throw, trade.

humiliation（n.）

❖ 例句

She will have to live with the humiliation of her rape if you don't help her.

如果你不幫助她，她就得一直活在被強暴的羞辱中。

The President accepted the humiliation of public penance, trying to save his political career.
總統為了想保住他的政治生涯而願意接受公開悔過的恥辱。

❖ 常用搭配詞

adj. + humiliation

public, this, final, national, total, such, further, ultimate, intense, greatest, own, past, second, ideological, deep, diplomatic, military.

v. +humiliation

mean, know, suffer, face, bring.

disgrace（n.）

❖ 例句

He is considered a disgrace to his family.
他被視為他家庭的恥辱。

It is an absolute disgrace that a new stadium should have so many defects in its drainage systems.
一個新體育館的排水系統有這麼多缺失真是丟臉。

❖ 常用搭配詞

adj. + disgrace

absolute, national, bloody, public, utter, royal, great, final, total, downright, damned.

v. + disgrace
  bring, mean, know, bear.

stigma（n.）

❖ 例句

There is a social stigma attached to obesity.
一般社會大眾把肥胖視為羞恥。

❖ 常用搭配詞

v. + the stigma of
  remove, suffer.

adj. + stigma
  social, proprietary, same.

綜合整理

shame	不可數名詞。因為自己或自己的親友做錯事而感到羞恥感或罪惡感。另外也指可惜的事情。
insult	可數名詞。冒犯他人或故意粗魯的言行舉止。
humiliation	不可數名詞。因為顯得愚蠢或軟弱而覺得羞辱或尷尬。
disgrace	不可數名詞。因為做錯事而失去他人的尊敬。
stigma	社會賦予的恥辱。

Unit 31 限制

StringNet語料庫出現次數

limit	restrict	confine	circumscribe
6543	3919	2656	124

limit（vt.）

❖ 常用句型

> **S + limit + O/反身代名詞 + to N**

❖ 例句

Campaign expenditure was limited to a maximum of NT$ 80,000,000 per candidate.
每位候選人的競選開銷上限是台幣八千萬元。

When trying out perfumes, I usually limit myself to three; after that , I 'll become 'fragrance blind'.
當我在嘗試香水時，我通常限制在三種香水，再多我就無法分辨香味了。

❖ 常用搭配詞

n.（s）+ be limited

space, places, resources, liability, choice, members, power, time, members, options, use, discussion, practice, appeal, activity, supply, value, area, opportunities, scope, information, policy, system, support, authority, jurisdiction, section, study, company, effects, impact, knowledge, development, range, funds, courts, school, debate, understanding, experience, market, rights, damage, applications, production, accommodation, service, data, interests, distance, capacity, output, risk, tickets, movement, flexibility, females, control, economy, size.

adv. + limit

severely, strictly, extremely, necessarily, usually, somewhat, normally, fairly, generally, largely, seriously, always, currently, probably, inevitably, increasingly, clearly, obviously, deliberately, considerably, initially, mainly, actually, effectively, socially, highly, significantly, drastically, comparatively, geographically, sufficiently, entirely, equally, naturally, originally, intrinsically, eventually, presently, substantially, ultimately.

limited to + n.

£1,000, cases, members, disclosure, items, decisions, exclusion, 10%, areas, proposals, companies, sex, defence, representatives, goods, documents, events.

restrict（vt.）

❖ 常用句型

> **S + restrict + O/反身代名詞 + to + N**
> **S + restrict + 反身代名詞 + to Ving**

❖ 例句

Many cities in Taiwan have restricted smoking in public parks.
台灣有許多城市限制在公共公園吸菸。

We should restrict the size of a language class to 20 students.
我們應該把語言課程的學生人數限制在20人。

❖ 常用搭配詞

n.（s）+ be restricted

movements, work, information, choice, section, use, activity, access, appeal, items, study, credit, samples, numbers, system, entry, tumor, life, expression, output, competition, facilities, sleep, family, claim, therapy, space, theory, service, powers, flow, means, capacity, attention, supply, territory, speed, growth, range, circulation, file.

adv. + restrict

severely, largely, usually, effectively, greatly, mainly, unduly, generally, seriously, necessarily, normally, increasingly, deliberately, probably, previously, highly, relatively, recently, simply, narrowly, apparently, hitherto, currently, inevitably, solely, heavily, clearly, artificially, obviously, correspondingly, progressively, sharply, actually, ultimately, systematically, entirely, substantially, regionally, gradually, mildly, equally, considerably, legally, surprisingly, radically, traditionally.

restrict to + n.

members, cases, patients, areas, issues, group, men, individuals, computer, graduates, residents, buses, specialists, animals, science, Britain, subjects, users.

confine（vt.）

❖ 常用句型

> **S + confine + O/反身代名詞 + to +N**
> **S + confine + 反身代名詞 + to Ving**

❖ 例句

These difficulties are most obvious in Asia, but they are not confined to it.
這些問題在亞洲最明顯，但不僅限於亞洲。

I shall confine myself to discussing only two of the examples.
我在此只討論其中兩個例子。

He has sprained his ankle and is confined to home.
他扭到腳踝了，只能待在家。

❖ 常用搭配詞

  n. (s) + be not confined to
   problem, experience, rule, practice, activity, dizziness, illustration, behavior, expression, war, life, policy, effect, principle.

  n. (s) + be confined to
   work, study, infection, life, discussion, judiciary, liability, effects, crypts, activity, research, struggle, problem, benefits, experience, feature, troops, service, breeding, company, convention, rule, analysis, education, information, conversation, remit.

adv. + confine

merely, better.

confine to + n.

bed, cases, women, barracks, Britain, people, members, London, men, home, hospital, males, areas, business, works, birds, restaurants, cells, employees, art, patients, adults, wheelchairs.

circumscribe（vt.）

❖ 常用句型

S + be circumscribed

❖ 例句

His powers are somewhat circumscribed by the tradition and local governments.

他的權力多多少少被傳統和地方政府所限制。

❖ 常用搭配詞

n.（s）+ be circumscribed

life, power, headteacher, future, plan, time, opportunity.

adv. + circumscribed

severely, narrowly, spatially.

綜合整理

limit	限制事物的增加、發展、或做想做的事情。受詞通常不是人，若是人的話則是反身代名詞表示自我限制。常用被動語態，limit 常加ed變成形容詞（如limited powers有限的權力）。
restrict	限制範圍、數量、大小等，或限制人的活動，常用在法律或規則上的限制（如legally restrict, traditionally restrict）。常用被動語態。
confine	限制活動範圍或主題，如拘禁，也指限制不好的事情擴散出去。受詞通常不是人，若是人的話則是反身代名詞表示自我限制。常用在否定被動語態，且主詞（受事者）是負面意義的事物（如 The problem is not fined to Asia這個問題不僅限於亞洲）。
circumscribe	正式用字。限制權力，能力，權利等，和restrict相似。通常用在被動語態。

Unit 32 相反的

StringNet語料庫出現次數

opposite	contrary	reverse	inverse
3124	1627	701	232

opposite（adj.）

❖ 例句

The bank is in the opposite direction to the supermarket.

那銀行和那家超市是反在方向。

❖ 常用搭配詞

opposite + n.

direction, side, sex, effect, number, end, way, page, wall, bank, extreme, sign, view, corner, knee, pole, shore, conclusion, problem, reason, case, pavement, sense, seat, point, party, result, orientation, line, wing, course, slope, pattern, charges, hemisphere, trend, kind, tendency, gender, bed, approach, reaction, angles, policies, hand, shoulder, stance, door, style, top, phase, principle, impression, coast, processes, argument, currents, position, reasons, function, field, condition, force, prediction, movement, passengers, feelings, states, symptoms, window, route, assumption, types, behavior, hillside, words, boundary, situation, bias, status, color, treatment, branch, virtues.

contrary（adj.）

❖ 例句

He went to his homeroom teacher, who gave him contrary advice.
他去找他的導師，他的導師給他相反的建言。
The new policy is contrary to the interest of the low-income households.
這項新政策違反低收入家庭的利益。

❖ 常用搭配詞

contrary + n.

   view, intention, agreement, themes, evidence, motion, indication,
   direction, effect, winds, advice, opinions, trend, nature, argument, sense,
   impression, results, proposition, relation, orientations, findings, results,
   decision, approaches, feelings, case, orders, conclusion, position, data.

reverse（adj.）

❖ 例句

The contents of the album are printed on the reverse side of the CD box.
這張專輯的內容印在盒的背面。
Reverse discrimination is discrimination against members of a dominant
group.
反向歧視的意義是歧視強勢族群的成員。
She knew that that would be what she would feel if the roles were reversed.
她知道如果角色對調她也會有相同的感受。

❖ 常用搭配詞

reverse + n.

punch, side, order, transcriptase, direction, takeover, osmosis, effect, gear, process, engineering, pattern, discrimination, situation, phase, flow, thrust, image, variable, roundhouse, transfer, case, primer, premium, transition, action, head, polarity, gearbox, video, turning, pivot, way, procedure, phenomenon, condition, yield, headstock, indemnity, movement, operation, reaction, sweep, bearing, influence, argument, discourse, swing, curve.

inverse（adj.）

❖ 例句

The experiment showed a significant inverse correlation between disability and social contact.
實驗結果顯示身心障礙的程度和社會接觸的程度呈現顯著負相關。

❖ 常用搭配詞

inverse + n.

relationships, proportion, relation, correlation, function, irreversibility, time, video, care, iteration, transformation, association, square, operation, ratio, intensity.

綜合整理

opposite	剛好完全相反的，尤其是二個相反或相對的人事物（如opposite page對面書頁，opposite sex異性）。後面接的名詞時常是方向、空間或方式。後面常接介系詞to。
contrary	不同的或相反的。後面名詞較常是心思意念、行動、性質。後面常接介系詞to。
reverse	位置（如if the roles were reversed如果角色對調）、程序或順序（如reverse process 相反程序）、方向（如reverse side反面，reverse gear倒退檔，reverse charges對方付費電話）等的相反。後面不接介系詞。
inverse	常用在數學用語（如inverse proportion成反比的，inverse correlation負相關的）。

另外adverse也有方向相反的意義，但是其主要的意義是不利的、敵對的、違背的等意義，表示相反方向只有少數用語（如adverse current逆流），因此在此不討論。

Unit 33 欣喜，愉快

StringNet語料庫出現次數

pleasure	joy	delight	ecstasy	bliss	euphoria	elation
5567	3116	2036	631	384	244	153

pleasure（n.）

❖ 例句

It's always a pleasure to attend a wedding. 參加婚禮總是令人愉快的。

❖ 常用搭配詞

the pleasure of + Ving

meeting, seeing, having, doing, working, walking, attending, feeling, knowing, watching, listening, taking, hearing, saying, going, riding, traveling, reading, using, getting, experiencing, playing.

adj. + pleasure

great, much, real, sexual, more, sheer, any, particular, enormous, little, pure, sensual, intense, physical, aesthetic, dubious, considerable, obvious, personal, visual, genuine, immense, perverse, private, simple, main, added, shared, endless, innocent, wild, malicious, small, apparent, special, driving, tremendous, quiet, vicarious, momentary, evident, deep, harmless, sweet, solid, sadistic, sensuous, forbidden, perverted, extraordinary, extra, total, good, anticipated, exquisite, lasting, additional, illicit, immediate, savage, emotional.

joy（n.）

❖ 例句

That Harley Davison is his pride and joy.
那台哈雷機車是他的驕傲和喜悅。

❖ 常用搭配詞

be a joy to + Vroot

  watch, see, listen, work, behold, do, drive, use, produce, walk.

adj. + joy

  great, sheer, much, little, more, pure, real, any, Christian, all, that, holy, overwhelming, inner, true, deep, delirious, wild, simple, double, obvious, sudden, incredulous, savage, fierce, secret, wonderful, genuine, physical, ecstatic, utter, perfect, fearful, exquisite, unexpected, perverse, rare, brief, full, mingled, spiritual, intense, inexpressible.

delight（n.）

❖ 例句

To the delight of his parents, he agreed to go to medical school.
令他父母高興的是他同意去讀醫學院。

❖ 常用搭配詞

be a delight to + Vroot

  see, have, watch, read, follow, behold, welcome, fly.

adj. + delight

great, sheer, culinary, pure, double, obvious, real, unexpected, perverse, particular, evident, sensual, absolute, earthly, endless, simple, visual, wild, scenic, aesthetic, spiritual, utter, childish, remembered, unrestrained, intense, positive, heady, deep, peculiar, mischievous, constant, unbearable, mutual, astonished, painful, incredulous, sweet, rapturous, profound, exquisite, sexual, cerebral, greedy, frequent, extra, unfeigned, immense, secret, wicked, innocent, continual, true, childlike, exuberant, dubious, sudden, unholy, physical, sensuous, rural.

ecstasy（n.）

❖ 例句

The wedded ecstasy was soon replaced by the hardship of real life.
新婚的狂喜很快就被現實生活的艱困所取代。

❖ 常用搭配詞

adj. + ecstasy

religious, sheer, real, sexual, sweet, spiritual, distorted, divine, pure, mystical.

the + n. of ecstasy

kind, tablets, worth, land, moment, visions, state, tears, dangers, discovery, sensation, peak.

bliss（n.）

❖ 例句

The bliss of Heaven filled her whenever she hears this hymn.
每當她聽到這首聖詩，她心中充滿天堂的喜樂。

❖ 常用搭配詞

adj. + bliss

　domestic, wedded, sheer, marital, married, absolute, pure, unadulterated, heavenly, straightforward, eternal, connubial, rural.

euphoria（n.）

❖ 例句

After the euphoria of the day when her long-lost son finally went back home came the hangover as she tried to work out what to do with his gambling debt.
經過她失聯多年的兒子終於回家的短暫喜悅後，她開始苦惱如何處理她兒子的賭債。

❖ 常用搭配詞

adj. + euphoria

　general, initial, current, alternating, eve-of-election.

the euphoria of the + n.

　moment, surprise, summer.

elation（n.）

❖ 例句

A feeling of elation took hold of the child when he climbed aboard the cruise.

當這孩子登上郵輪時心中充滿了興奮喜悅。

❖ 常用搭配詞

a + n. of elation

　　sense, feeling, state, surge, mixture, mood, moment.

adj. + elation

　　sheer, joyous, unbelievable, mild, new.

綜合整理

pleasure	喜悅、滿足，尤其是在某個活動或經驗當中的愉快感覺。常用在 have pleasure in + Ving, take great pleasure in + Ving 等片語。
joy	強烈的喜樂、歡樂、或樂事。
delight	高興、滿足、欣喜。片語to the delight of somebody表示令某人高興的事情發展。常用在take great delight in Ving 和take a + adj. + delight in + Ving 等片語。
ecstasy	狂喜，吸毒或性行為造成的興奮（如drug ecstasy），或宗教的出神入迷狀態。
bliss	極致的幸福感或興奮（如wedded bliss新婚之樂），像在天堂一般精神上的喜樂。另外也表示福氣。
euphoria	短暫的狂喜。
elation	快樂、興奮的感覺，尤其因為某件事情的發生。

Unit 34 行為

StringNet語料庫出現次數

act	conduct	deed	behavior
24594	2912	1248	81

act（n.）

❖ 例句

The government will not tolerate such a criminal act.

政府絕不包容如此犯罪行為。

❖ 常用搭配詞

adj. + act

unlawful, sexual, double, criminal, wrongful, illegal, deliberate, individual, political, violent, negligent, homosexual, positive, mental, public, physical, creative, symbolic, social, aggressive, great, willful, conscious, voluntary, unilateral, juggling, careless, altruistic, lawful, unauthorized, hostile, isolated, barbaric, despicable, humanitarian, disappearing, surrender, outrageous, generous, dangerous, appalling, inhuman, giant-killing, immoral, impulsive, unfriendly, indecent, alleged, unreasonable, trivial, anti-social, anti-apartheid, stupid, dramatic, strange, evil, intentional, subsequent, serious, forbidden, controversial, dreadful, magic, extreme, deviant.

conduct（n.）

❖ 例句

No charges of breaching the Code of Professional Conduct were ever brought.
從來沒有人因為違反職業道德準則而被起訴。

❖ 常用搭配詞

adj. + conduct

professional, such, sexual, human, violent, good, future, proper, disorderly, safe, improper, personal, offensive, criminal, homosexual, aggressive, oppressive, actual, efficient negligent, unlawful, illegal, official, ungentlemanly, ethical, discreditable, political, unreasonable, day-to-day, unethical, subsequent, dishonest, wrongful, prejudicial, unconscionable, fraudulent, moral, dishonorable, bad, individual, exemplary, irresponsible, successful, tortious, immoral, abusive, civilized, permissible, unjustifiable, public, brave, financial, rational, irregular, social, peaceful, meritorious, outrageous, deviant, rude, usual.

deed（n.）

❖ 例句

They could not keep quiet about the mighty deeds of God.
關於上帝的大能作為他們不能緘默不說。

❖ 常用搭配詞

adj. + deed

　good, evil, great, such, dark, heroic, brave, mighty, dirty, dastardly, noble, past, foul, terrible, glorious, stirring, daring, charitable, nefarious, virtuous, wrongful, miraculous, unnatural, bloody.

behavior（n.）

❖ 例句

Is it possible to deduce human behavior from the laws of science?
有可能以科學的法則來推斷人類的行為嗎?
He is writing a report about the voting behavior of citizens under the age of 30.
他在寫一篇有關三十歲以下市民投票行為的報導。

❖ 常用搭配詞

adj. + behavior

　human, learned.

綜合整理

act	單一一次的行為。當名詞時還有其他多種意義，所以在語料庫出現次數極多。
conduct	一個人的行為舉止，尤其指在工作上或公開場合從道德倫理角度看待的行為。
deed	單一一次的行為或一般行為。正式用字，前面常接good或bad等正評或負評的形容詞。當名詞時也表示證書或契據，法律用字。
behavior	人或動物的習性行為，或某件事物的運作方式。在語料庫出現次數很少。

另外demeanor指反映某人個性或感受的行為舉止（如Every time you mentioned his name, Julia's demeanor changed.每次你提到他的名字，Julia的舉止就和往常不同）。因為語料庫沒收錄，所以在此不列入。

Unit 35 性質，特質

StringNet語料庫出現次數

quality	nature	property	character	attribute
18633	17881	16557	12296	2285

quality（n.）

❖ 例句

The quality and quantity of the language input is essential to the success of language acquisition.
語言習得的成功取決於語言輸入的質和量。

❖ 常用搭配詞

v. + quality

improve, have, provide, produce, assess, make, deliver, sacrifice, ensure, guarantee, maintain, get, need, establish, raise, determine, promote, achieve, define, monitor, appreciate, meet, measure, judge, affect, enhance, select, control, pursue, lack, develop, specify, secure.

adj. + quality

high, good, poor, top, total, personal, merchantable, special, environmental, low, particular, internal, essential, superior, fine, outstanding, important, aesthetic, overall, positive, unique, exceptional, variable, individual, intrinsic, acceptable, specific, acoustic, negative, bad, consistent, desirable, architectural, rare, average, physical, spiritual, natural, admirable, abstract, primary, distinctive, magical, dynamic, vital, timeless, comparable, universal, original, managerial, actual, equal, useful, underlying, dubious.

n. + quality

water, air, product, service, teaching, recording, voice, output, food, data, print, reservoir, river, image, land, research, broadcast, soil, software, health, design, student,

nature（n.）

❖ 例句

Human conversation is reciprocal in nature.
人類對話的本質是交互的。

❖ 常用搭配詞

the nature of the + n.

relationship, work, problem, state, business, act, task, job, contract, world, information, transaction, subject, offence, evidence, process, case, power, changes, product, goods, material, object, company, interaction, disease, experience, event, research, war, services, terrain, soil, document, stimulus, crime, data, society, partnership, enterprise, dispute, premises, community, land, environment, activities, organization, risk, exercise, action, industry, rock, scheme, cause, fault, family, game, phenomena, universe, role, revolution.

<u>adj.</u> + nature

true, precise, exact, changing, general, different, complex, similar, specific, essential, physical, real, divine, social, sexual, confidential, temporary, intrinsic, whole, contradictory, dynamic, basic, fundamental, chemical, legal, practical, distinctive, unique, abstract, problematic, subjective, sensitive, spiritual, dual, actual, peculiar, unusual, individual, interactive, historical, ideological, controversial, adversarial, interdisciplinary, religious, economic, arbitrary, paradoxical, traditional, uncertain, progressive, commercial, unpredictable, crucial, symbolic, complementary, systematic, diverse, transient, pluralistic, financial, open-ended, dubious, experimental, benign, heterogeneous, volatile, static, universal, psychological, addictive, democratic, unchanging, variable, divided, delicate, rudimentary, cumbersome, speculative, vague, ambiguous, permanent, chronic, hazardous, pragmatic, elusive, ultimate, reciprocal, independent, academic, technological, two-way, theoretical, regressive, fragile, substantial, hereditary, temporal, ephemeral, explosive, discontinuous, multi-cultural, linear, advisory, fleeting, primitive, uncontrolled, diffuse.

property（n.）

❖ 例句

He doesn't trust the healing properties of Chinese herbs.
他不信任中藥藥草的療效。

❖ 常用搭配詞

adj. + property

   intrinsic, physical, unusual, natural, chemical, underlying, emergent, semantic, hereditary, pleasant, mysterious, fundamental.

character（n.）

❖ 例句

The whole character of school education has changed due to low birth rate.
少子化已經改變了學校教育的本質。

❖ 常用搭配詞

the character of the + adj. + n.

   area, building, part, mode.

adj. + character

   essential, general, unique, original, changing, social, complex, whole, historic, true, historical, traditional, overall, interesting, similar, volatile, economic, medieval, unusual, dynamic, academic, industrial, fundamental, basic, distinct, natural, varied, abstract, legal, architectural, primitive, actual, idiosyncratic, multidisciplinary, homogeneous, obligatory, radical, permanent, intrinsic, alternative, normal, contradictory, universal, ideological, consistent, ethnic, temporal.

attribute（n.）

❖ 例句

She possesses all the essential attributes of a good mother.
她具有一個好母親的所有特質。

Most men are drawn more by the physical attributes of a woman than the quality of her personality.
大部分男性被一個女性的外表吸引多於她的個性。

❖ 常用搭配詞

adj. + attribute

physical, these, other, personal, human, important, main, essential, this, particular, positive, necessary, common, divine, social, desirable, various, each, possible, cultural, specific, psychological, natural, relevant, distinctive, functional, certain, mental, related, individual, sexual, sensory, useful, moral, negative, basic, feminine, given, similar, associated, greatest, semantic.

attributes of the + n.

entity, product, company, nation

綜合整理

quality	某事物本身特有的性質，相對於quantity（數量）。前面常接good, bad, high, low等形容詞來評斷品質的優劣，of quality 指優良的品質。
nature	事物的本質、特色，也指人的性情。
property	物質或植物的性質或能力。和quality相似。較常表示個人財產的意義。
character	某事物或某地方整體的特質。和nature相似。較常表示個人品行或戲劇角色的意義。
attribute	人事物的特質，有正面意義，指美好的或有用的特質。

Unit 36 執照，證書

StringNet語料庫出現次數

license	certificate	diploma	credentials
4354	3706	901	369

license（n.）

❖ 例句

Have you got a driving license?

你有駕照嗎？

❖ 常用搭配詞

n. + license

driving, television, excise, export, hotel, entertainment, user, restaurant, trade, house, canteen, import, software, fund, marriage, disposal, refreshment, operating, product, drinks, music, film, prospecting, radio, development, bar, liquor, server, network, operator, mark, car, parole, government, gun, banking, source, pilots, vehicle, trading, sale, broadcasting, Microsoft, hunting, desktop, Texas, bookseller, investment, transport, safety, business, franchise, ministry, credit, lease, boxing, gambilng, patent.

license + n.

fee, holder, agreement, application, sales, number, revenues, system, money, manager, conditions, payers, management, plates, final, packs, areas, dodger, auction, interests, blocks, center, charges, obligations, trade, renewal, stamps, awards, distinction, duty, record, price.

adj. + license

new, all, existing, necessary, provisional, offshore, royal, current, off-sale, industrial, temporary, individual.

v. + license

grant, obtain, revoke, have, peddle, hold, auction, issue.

certificate（n.）

❖ 例句

Have you applied for a birth certificate for your baby?
你幫你的寶寶申請出生證明了嗎?

❖ 常用搭配詞

n. + certificate

birth, death, school, test, marriage, postgraduate, share, aid, land, insurance, audit, charge, banking, remuneration, tax, hygiene, fire, maternity, assistant, service, proficiency, representation, teaching, business, mortgage, access, exemption, education, entry, skills, safety, completion, loan, post-graduate, award, craft, immunity, accreditation, prize, university, development, quality, management, teachers, membership, discharge, wine, merit, graduate, adoption, association, course, foundation, export, firearm, health, training, coaching, virgin, burial, hotel, college, design, power, payment, savings.

adj. + certificate

national, practicing, professional, general, first, medical, advanced, framed, interim, official, second, new, preliminary, relevant, first-class, full, final, signed, school-leaving, part-time, valid, additional, retail, provisional, separate, fresh, original, existing, previous, compact, nationally-recognized, technological, amended, necessary, free, standard, introductory, appropriate, qualifying, unconditional, single, green, work-based, required.

v. + a certificate

have, receive, obtain, award, issue, get, sign, present, grant, get, require, produce, give, win, gain, deliver, refuse, request.

diploma（n.）

❖ 例句

If you want to get a good job, try to get a college diploma.
如果你想要找一個好工作，就設法拿到大學文憑。

❖ 常用搭配詞

n. + diploma

postgraduate, graduate, polytechnic, trustee, university, studies, dance, college, post-graduate, management, company, government, school.

diploma + n.

course, program, level, students, examinations, holders, membership.

adj. + diploma

national, professional, higher, advanced, two-year, first, final, post-experience, new, full-time, first-class, full, impressive, external, qualifying.

v. + a diploma

have, obtain, award, take, hold, get, receive.

credentials（n.）

❖ 例句

Despite his impressive credentials as a professor, he was not hired by the university.

雖然他有身為教授亮眼的學經歷，這個大學沒有聘用他。

❖ 常用搭配詞

adj. + credentials

academic, democratic, green, educational, scientific, impeccable, conservative, socialist, impressive, right, diplomatic, perfect, good, financial, international, reformist, philosophical, political, environmental, excellent, empirical, liberal, ideal, European, Islamic.

v. + one's credentials

present, establish, check.

綜合整理

license	可數名詞。被准許擁有某物或做某事的執照，通常有時間限制（如 renew a license更新執照）。在商業上則是指某公司或機構所給予買賣或製造他們商品的執照。
certificate	可數名詞。證明某個事實的證書（如birth certificate出生證明），也指完成課程或通過考試的證書。
diploma	可數名詞。在美式英文指畢業證書，在英式英文指完成課程或通過考試的證書。也表示獎狀或公文。
credentials	複數名詞。證明某人有某種技能的教育背景、成就、經驗等的證明文件，也指某職位的資格證明書。

Unit 37 主要的

StringNet語料庫出現次數

main	primary	chief	principal
24392	8498	7418	3963

main（adj.）

❖ 例句

The main body of the hurricane has moved south.
這個颶風的主體已經往南移。

❖ 常用搭配詞

main + n.

road, reason, line, problem, street, concern, thing, areas, aim, points, opposition, source, purpose, entrance, body, types, features, building, parties, part, course, thrust, picture, cause, difference, theme, objective, task, issues, hall, categories, function, factors, ways, door, meal, house, character, elements, route, effect, interest, bed, classes, event, menu, attraction, carriage, area, argument, outcome, advantage, square, storage, force, role, emphasis, office, characteristics, subject, centers, components, room, form, residence, beneficiaries, target, methods, sections, question, work, findings, topic, proceedings, news, text, changes, clause, rival, responsibility, conclusions, priority, bedroom, difficulty, stream, staircase, principles, market, idea, obstacle, database, stages, aspects, library, contract, cities, item, field, criterion, message, survey, threat, story, ingredient, contenders, research, power, runway, consideration, branches, enemy, artery, support, island, complaint, trends, corridor, theories, goal, competitor, claim, station, protagonists, fuel, frame, weakness, candidates, stems, motivation, products, value, sponsor, impetus, customers, victims, culprit, challenge, outlines, requirement, policy, speaker, weapon, deck, provider, agenda, crop, need, fear.

primary（adj.）

❖ 例句

The primary aim of the foundation is to secure the future of the rainforest.
這個基金會的主要目標是要確保雨林的未來。

❖ 常用搭配詞

primary + n.

discipline, school, subject, care, education, health, purpose, sufferer, source, aim, concern, teachers, objective, function, level, color, role, responsibility, importance, legislation, elections, data, task, cause, prevention, sector, process, focus, reason, interest, curriculum, site, disease, industries, products, duty, market, goal, phase, directory, consideration, street, emphasis, antibody, evidence, stage, rules, motivation, need, commodities, energy, goods, lesion, functions, infection, forest, target, course, research, survey, diagnosis, circuit, problem, gall, treatment, submission, motive, structure, meaning, force, attack, factor, area, language, resource, health-care.

chief（adj.）

❖ 例句

He is the chief executive of a non-profit organization.
他是一家非營利組織的執行長。

❖ 常用搭配詞

chief + n.

executive, inspector, minister, secretary, officer, engineer, whip, superintendent, steward, economist, designer, scientist, rabbi, clerk, negotiator, agent, architect, reason, planning, concern, adviser, judge, coach, source, rival, instructor, scout, suspect, bridesmaid, administrator, librarian, cause, interest, problem, assistant curator, spokesman, aim, purpose, coordinator, character, manager, objective, opponent, function, reporter, factor, priest, union, warden, editor, instrument, responsibility, sponsor, target, advantage, surgeon, difference, fund-raiser, investment, attraction, enemy.

principal（adj.）

❖ 例句

The reservoir serves as the principal source of drinking water for this region.
這個水庫是這地區飲用水的主要來源。

❖ 常用搭配詞

principal + n.

> trading, ministers, source, reason, place, method, concern, aim, members, objective, components, repayments, means, focus, features, officers, carers, areas, factor, career, purpose, forms, investigators, inspector, cause, problem, role, types, subject, adviser, task, actors, advantage, element, opposition, characters, part, theme, target, interest, residence, architect, ways, author, difference, products.

綜合整理

main	同類事物或想法中最大的或最重要的，和chief相似。後面接的名詞包含建築物（如building, cities）、道路（如road, street）、困難（如difficulty, threat）、意念（如goal, motivation）等類，如果是表示人的名詞通常是指主要互動的人群或單位（如provider供應商，customers顧客）。
primary	最首要的、首先的、或是最重要的，和chief和main相似。常用在和小學教育（如primary school）和醫療（如primary care, primary treatment）相關的名詞片語。
chief	等級最高、最首要的、最重要的。後面名詞時常是職位（如chief executive, chief engineer），表示首席的、主要的職位。
principal	最首要的或是最重要的，和chief和main相似。

Unit 38 注意的，留意的

StringNet語料庫出現次數

intent	attentive	mindful
1259	238	174

intent（adj.）

❖ 例句

She was intent on reading the novel that she didn't hear the doorbell.
她專心在看小說，以至於沒聽到門鈴聲。

❖ 常用搭配詞

be intent on + Ving

　　making, getting, ensuring, breaking, taking, pursuing, bringing, exploiting, creating, killing, isolating, becoming, keeping, finding, playing.

attentive（adj.）

❖ 例句

We are impressed by your attentive service.
我們對你們的服務周到感到印象深刻。

❖ 常用搭配詞

attentive + n.

　　service, listener, reader.

attentive to（det.）+ <u>n.</u>

  needs, safety, legislature, point, object, game, need.

mindful（adj.）

❖ 例句

Every personnel should be mindful of the dangers of revealing personal information.

每位員工都應該注意洩漏個資的危險。

❖ 常用搭配詞

mindful of the + <u>n.</u>

  fact, need, dangers, predicament.

綜合整理

intent	專心注意，心無旁鶩的。後面常接介系詞on。
attentive	因為感到有興趣而專注地聽或看，也指留意別人的需要。後面常接介系詞to。
mindful	有查覺到的，留意的，也指留意別人的需要。後面常接介系詞of。

Unit 39 狀況

StringNet語料庫出現次數

state	condition	situation	status
43497	23509	19544	8662

state（n.）

❖ 例句

She is unhappy and frustrated at the vague, unsettled state of their relationship.
她為了他們之間曖昧不明且不穩定的關係感到不快樂和挫折。

The way you breathe reflects your emotional and mental states.
你呼吸的方式會反應你的情感以及心理狀態。

❖ 常用搭配詞

adj. + state

mental, new, present, current, steady, solid, emotional, poor, different, individual, natural, psychological, terrible, existing, fit, initial, sensory, particular, certain, bad, inner, depressed, original, normal, advanced, financial, stable, permanent, previous, excited, possible, right, sad, open, neutral, vegetative, ideal, fasting, real, final, confused, nutritional, better, unsatisfactory, appalling, disturbed, distressed, hypnotic, common, economic, ideological, populous, weakened, liquid, dreadful,, disordered, wild, perpetual, actual, dangerous, spiritual, worse, repressive, internal, unhappy, secular, political, autonomous, chaotic, desirable, naive, protected, critical, past, anxious, limited, negative, diabetic, conscious, early, nervous, whole, married, reasonable, serious, uncertain, approved.

condition（n.）

❖ 例句

Your flight is delayed because of poor weather conditions.
你的班機因為天候不佳而延遲。
All the sedans we hire are in excellent condition.
我們租的轎車車況都非常好。

❖ 常用搭配詞

n. + conditions

working, weather, market, water, prison, housing, employment, road, soil, ground, wind, winter, traffic, wartime, lighting, business, laboratory, drought, sea, health, driving, heart, work, snow, skin, classroom, viewing, war, temperature, labor, living, licence, blizzard, life, flight, home, booking, credit, visibility, culture, climate, room, storm, peacetime, flood.

adj. + condition

good, excellent, physical, poor, human, medical, immaculate, perfect, mental, critical, original, stable, present, pristine, better, bad, serious, worse, flying, social, common, superb, clinical, special, neutral, terrible, chronic, financial, natural, structural, nervous, psychological, satisfactory, economic,normal, dangerous, current, life-threatening, distressing, overall, emotional, unusual, possible, unstable, prior, crucial, rare, comfortable, temporary, appalling, healthy, visual, static, painful, psychiatric, sanitary, initial, fatal, pathological, decent, right.

situation（n.）

❖ 例句

He was faced with a situation where he would be either hurt or embarrassed.
他面臨不是被傷害就是很尷尬的狀況。

The situation was complicated by the intervention of the outsider.
外人的介入使得情況更複雜。

❖ 常用搭配詞

adj. + situation

economic, present, political, current, particular, financial, similar, difficult, whole, social, given, different, real, own, dangerous, international, intolerable, ideal, impossible, complex, military, general, actual, serious, local, competitive, embarrassing, historical, awkward, desperate, personal, stressful, bad, hypothetical, common, immediate, unusual, domestic, existing, unsatisfactory, no-win, terrible, contemporary, complicated, specific, deteriorating, typical, legal, practical, extraordinary, tense, ludicrous, unique, worsening, normal, ridiculous, overall, strange, bizarre, tricky, odd, following, interesting, hopeless, explosive, real-live, right, confused, critical, appalling, paradoxical, extreme, tragic, disastrous, possible, desirable, socio-economic, good, earlier, painful, absurd, precise, unhappy, reverse, delicate, unstable.

n. + situation

security, market, work, family, employment, learning, home, life, supply, emergency, war, teaching, classroom, problem, interview, speech, conflict, housing, business, language, job, monopoly, egg, hostage, status, school, refugee, sell, fire, design, good, loss, injury, tax.

status（n.）

❖ 例句

You will be asked questions about your age, sex, race, and marital status.
你們會被問到關於你們的年齡、性別、種族、和婚姻狀況等問題。
You should be concerned about the nutritional status of your diet when trying to lose weight.
當你在減重的時候應該要注意你攝取食物的營養狀態。

❖ 常用搭配詞

adj. + status

marital, legal, current, economic, financial, political, independent, nutritional, occupational, corporate, overt, similar, different, future, moral, relative, smoking, active, autonomous, single, diplomatic, present, personal, permanent, protected, separate, educational, ambiguous, unique, neutral, precise, employed, married, whole, temporary, non-resident, real, ethnic.

n. + status

trust, health, software, employment, refugee, trading, class, company, division, tax, family, security, registration, dependence, approval, nutrient, commonwealth.

綜合整理

state	某個人或某件事物的身心狀況或某物質的狀況。在語料庫中大多表示國家或州郡,因此在語料庫出現次數很多。
condition	可數或不可數名詞。某個事物的狀況,尤其是好或壞的狀況,也指人的健康狀況。另外也表示條件,因此在語料庫出現次數很多。
situation	情況,情勢,某個特定時空之內發生的事情以及其環境的總組合。有時候有負面意義,前面時常出現負面意義的形容詞(如awkward, desperate, embarrassing等)。
status	情況、狀況,在法律上的狀態(如marital status婚姻狀態)。另外也指身分地位。

Unit 40 重要的

StringNet語料庫出現次數

important	significant	vital	crucial
38685	11980	5035	4403

important（adj.）

❖ 例句

He is one of the most important architects of the Victorian period.
他是維多利亞時期最重要的建築師之一。

❖ 常用搭配詞

important + _n._

part, thing, role, point, factor, aspect, feature, issue, things, element, source, question, contribution, implications, step, differences, consideration, changes, people, work, areas, influence, matter, decisions, respects, information, component, reason, development, consequences, distinction, place, business, fact, function, principle, effect, person, event, piece, sense, means, cause, problem, example, figure, ingredient, market, lesson, job, stage, item, resource, link, subject, book, exception, time, advantage, buildings, trading, insights, policy, variables, theme, message, form, case, collection, details, game, asset, positions, tool, indicator, debate, characteristics, finding, document, goal, statement, impact, study, topic, research, skill, focus, clue, criterion, dimension, qualification, section, aid, data, sites, gap, occasions, milestone, breakthrough, wildlife, material, property, benefits, discoveries, match, conclusion, victory.

significant（adj.）

❖ 例句

This new policy is significant for the future of the next generation.
這個新政策對於下一代的未來有重大影響。

❖ 常用搭配詞

significant + n.

difference, changes, part, number, increase, proportion, contribution, role, impact, effect, factor, improvement, amount, correlation, reduction, progress, degree, feature, development, growth, shift, step, extent, minority, loss, event, aspect, way, decline, advantage, harm, source, problem, rise, relationship, quantities, variations, advances, gains, risk, benefits, scale, move, breakthrough, interaction, stake, level, results, achievement, force, exception, support, threat, trend, cost, measure, expansion, implications, gap, contributor, challenge, cause, work, potential, issues, evidence, damage, consequences, victory.

vital（adj.）

❖ 例句

The heart, lungs, kidney and brain are vital organs in the human body.
心臟、肺臟、腎臟、以及腦部是人體維生的重要器官。

His vital signs were stable when he was found.
當他被發現時他的生命現象穩定。

❖ 常用搭配詞

vital + n.

part, role, importance, information, organs, element, ingredient, factor, statistics, signs, link, work, clue, force, component, points, interest, contribution, question, piece, evidence, supplies, source, thing, service, functions, resource, principle, area, need, aspect, issue, step, energy, support, difference, equipment, decisions, task, world, goal, research, fact, moment, food.

crucial（adj.）

❖ 例句

The crucial factor of this project is time.
這個計畫最關鍵的因素是時間。

❖ 常用搭配詞

crucial + n.

role, importance, factor, part, point, question, issue, difference, element, stage, time, moment, test, step, period, thing, distinction, decisions, aspect, decision, evidence, vote, area, information, feature, component, significance, problem, years, talks, function, link, influence, ones, respects, debate, contribution, ingredient, figure, phase, meeting, support, piece, change, victory, breakthrough, nature, passage, condition, event, place, need, matter, goals.

綜合整理

important	對某件事情的本質或未來發展有強大的影響。
significant	對未來將發生的事情有重要的影響。另外也表示相當（多）的。
vital	對某事物的成功或生存非常重要。和crucial相似。常表示維生所必須的或攸關生死的（如vital organs, vital food, vital signs）。後面的名詞不能是人。
crucial	是某件事情的關鍵因素。和vital相似。後面的名詞不能是人。

Unit 41 折磨

StringNet語料庫出現次數

torture	rack	torment
696	285	283

torture（n.）

❖ 例句

The bodies of the victims showed signs of torture.
受害者的遺體顯示曾經被折磨虐待。

❖ 常用搭配詞

adj. + torture

mental, physical, systematic, daily, brutal, worse, widespread, absolute, psychological, exquisite, human, subtle, sheer, real, indescribable, cruel.

rack（vt.）

❖ 例句

She was racked by a feeling of guilt.
她內心受到罪惡感的折磨。

He has racked his brains for an alternative.
他絞盡腦汁想找出替代方法。

❖ 常用搭配詞

be racked with + n.

pain, guilt, sobs, doubts.

torment（n.）

❖ 例句

She was tormented by jealousy.
她因忌妒飽受煎熬。

❖ 常用搭配詞

adj. + torment

mental, inner, private, subtle, strange, aching, everlasting, fiery.

綜合整理

torture	可當名詞或動詞，當動詞時常用被動語態，名詞的用法比較多。指極大肉體或精神的痛苦，尤其指為了逼供、處罰、或出於兇殘的折磨。
rack	動詞。使人遭受極大肉體或精神的痛苦。片語rack one's brain表示絞盡腦汁。
torment	可當名詞或動詞，較常表示精神上的折磨痛苦。和torture相似。

Unit 42 掙扎

StringNet語料庫出現次數

struggle	falter	flounder
3603	415	159

struggle（vi.）

❖ 常用句型

> S + struggle + to do something
> S + struggle + adv./ prep. + N

❖ 例句

People are struggling for survival.
大家都在掙扎求生存。

The footage of a Journalist struggling against strong wind seems to be a must in typhoon TV news.
颱風電視新聞報導似乎一定要有記者在強風中掙扎的鏡頭。

❖ 常用搭配詞

struggle to + Vroot

get, keep, find, make, survive, maintain, cope, control, hold, overcome, free, stay, come, retain, bring, contain, understand, put, do, sit, escape, pay, break, pull, achieve, recover, meet, remember, establish, reach, avoid, rise, regain, match, score, think, follow, learn, fill, preserve, create, balance, breathe, hide, express, stop, suppress, adapt, reconcile, emerge, raise, master, complete, catch, beat, gain, pass, lift, explain, fight.

struggle + adv.

desperately, financially, furiously, manfully, painfully, valiantly, constantly, fiercely, vainly, briefly, feebly, unavailingly, unsuccessfully, madly.

flounder（vi.）

❖ 常用句型

> **S + flounder + adv./ prep. + N**

❖ 例句

The life guard saw a man floundering furiously in the deep waters of the sea.
救生員看到在海中深處有一位男子在水中拼命挣扎。

❖ 常用搭配詞

flounder + adv.

around, helplessly, excitedly, furiously.

綜合整理

struggle	在困境中挣扎以達成某個目標，也表示挣扎前進、求生或逃脫等。
flounder	在水中或泥中挣扎前進，後面必須接副詞或介系詞。另外也指慌張失措。

Unit 43 征服，戰勝

StringNet語料庫出現次數

overcome	defeat	conquer	subdue
3312	3275	599	266

overcome（vt.）

❖ 常用句型

> **S + overcome +O**

❖ 例句

There are a number of ways of overcoming this problem.
有幾個方法可以用來克服這個問題。

❖ 常用搭配詞

overcome this + _n._

　problem, difficulty, hurdle, obstacle, barrier, deficiency, opposition.

overcome these + _n._

　problems, difficulties, obstacles, constraints, limitations, fears.

overcome the + _n._

　problem, effects, difficulties, division, limitations, obstacles, lack,
　resistance, forces, opposition, world, crisis, isolation, weakness, fear,

loss, capacity, barrier, elements, pain, disadvantages, friction, weakness, prejudices, challenge, constrainst.

defeat（vt.）

❖ 常用句型

> **S + defeat + O（by +N）**

❖ 例句

He is determined to defeat his opponent.
他決心要打敗他的對手。

❖ 常用搭配詞

n. + be defeated
   government, motion, army, amendment, proposal, fleet, Germany, rebels, motions, members, campaign, king, forces, party, unionism.

defeat the + n.
   government, rebels, power, witch.

conquer（vt.）

❖ 常用句型

> **S + conquer +O**

❖ 例句

We have conquered the most difficult part of the experiment.

我們已經克服了這個實驗最困難的部分。

After three days they finally conquered the peak of the mountain.

三天後他們終於攻頂成功。

❖ 常用搭配詞

conquer the + _n._

　world, rest, country, queen, island, north, peaks, land.

subdue（vt.）

❖ 常用句型

> **S + subdue + O**

❖ 例句

She managed to subdue her anger when she saw her ex-husband on the court.

當她在法庭上看見她的前夫，她設法壓抑她的憤怒。

He used pepper spray to subdue the burglar.

他用防身噴霧制服了闖空門的竊賊。

❖ 常用搭配詞

subdue the + _n._

　rebels, earth, spirit, island, tribes.

綜合整理

overcome	戰勝某種不好的感覺或問題以達成某件事情，或在比賽或戰爭中戰勝對方。用在被動時表示被某種情緒擊垮。
defeat	在戰爭或比賽中戰勝對方，常用被動句。另有使困惑不懂和使失敗的意思。
conquer	以武力征服國家，也指打敗敵人或克服困難。
subdue	制服或打敗一個或一群人。也指壓制自己的情緒使不外露。

Unit 44 拯救

StringNet語料庫出現次數

save	rescue	salvage
11763	1609	336

save（vt.）

❖ 常用句型

> **S + save + O（from + N）**

❖ 例句

In order to save her life the doctor had to amputate his left arm.
為了要救他的性命，醫生必須把他的左手臂截肢。
He has saved you from a long prison-term.
他救了你免於長期的牢獄之災。

❖ 常用搭配詞

save +（det.） n.

life, child, day, world, job, people, jobs, souls, England, mankind, democracy, children, sinners, China, animals, man, elephants, dolphins, trouble, school, Israel, day, baby, woman, Lisa（人名）, family, marriages, wildlife, car, civilization, buildings, lake, embarrassment, death, loss, home, faith, newspapers, Christianity.

recue（vt.）

❖ 常用句型

S + recue + O（from + N）

❖ 例句

Seventy people were rescued from the sinking ship.
有七十人從那艘快要沉沒的船上被救出來。
The new President introduced a government program to rescue the country's ailing economy.
這位新總統推出一套政府的計劃來拯救這個國家虛弱的經濟。

❖ 常用搭配詞

recue the + n.

country, economy, government, girl, hostages, prisoners, company, animals, men, princess, man, child, US, match, savings.

be rescued by + n.

helicopter, firemen, police, crewmen, boat, lifeboat, security.

be rescued from the + n.

river, sea, wreckage, threat, car, roof.

salvage（vt.）

❖ 常用句型

> **S + salvage + O（from + N）**

❖ 例句

He managed to salvage his papers from the fire.
他設法從火中搶救他的論文。

He tried hard to salvage his reputation.
他努力地想挽救他的名譽。

❖ 常用搭配詞

salvage +（det.）<u>n.</u>

  pride, consortium, aircraft, situation, something.

綜合整理

save	及物動詞，拯救人事物使其免於危險、毀滅、或傷害，受詞可以是人事物。另有節省、儲存等其他多種意義，當名詞時表示保險箱。
recue	及物動詞，也可以當名詞。從危險、傷害、困難、或不愉快的情境當中把人事物拯救出來，受詞可以是人事物。和save不大一樣，save是在事情還沒發生前預防其發生，而rescue則是事情已經發生後把人事物從其中救出來，因此救難隊是rescue team。
salvage	從意外或不利的處境搶救部分的物品或財產。受詞通常不是人。

Unit 45 稱讚

StringNet語料庫出現次數

praise	hail	commend	compliment	acclaim	extol
1486	777	616	201	151	151

praise（vt.）

❖ 常用句型

> **S + praise + O**

❖ 例句

This movie has been highly praised by movie critics.
這部電影受到影評家高度的稱讚。

❖ 常用搭配詞

n.（s） + be praised

report, God, saints, heavens, work.

praise the + n.

Lord, work, efforts, staff, police, courage, team, way, child, coroner, contribution, government, bravery, people, professionalism, care, duke, church, value, role, beauty, president, dog.

hail（vt.）

❖ 常用句型

> S + hail + somebody/something as something
> S + be hailed + something

❖ 例句

The sculpture has been hailed as a masterpiece.
這雕像被讚許為傑作。

❖ 常用搭配詞

be hailed as a (adj.) + n.

　success, hero, beginning, milestone, advance.

commend（vt.）

❖ 常用句型

> S + commend somebody（for something）
> S + be（adv.）commended

❖ 例句

The mayor commended the boy for his brave deeds.
市長稱讚這位小男孩的英勇事蹟。

❖ 常用搭配詞

adv. + commended

　highly, widely, especially, much.

compliment（vt.）

❖ 常用句型

> **S + compliment somebody（on something）**

❖ 例句

At the party he complimented Jessica on her beauty.
在派對上他稱讚Jessica的美貌。

❖ 常用搭配詞

v. + the compliment

　return, repay, deserve, acknowledge.

acclaim（vt.）

❖ 常用句型

> **S + acclaim + somebody/ something**
> **S + be acclaimed（as something）**

❖ 例句

His second book, which was widely acclaimed, established his international reputation.

他的第二本書廣受好評，建立了他的國際聲譽。

❖ 常用搭配詞

adv. + acclaimed

　highly, widely, critically, internationally, universally.

extol（vt.）

❖ 常用句型

> **S + extol + something**

❖ 例句

Adverts extolling his virtues were placed at every suitable vantage point.

對他歌功頌德的廣告被放在每一個制高點。

❖ 常用搭配詞

extol one's + n.

　virtues, genius, charm, beauty.

綜合整理

praise	崇拜或佩服某人或某件事情,尤其是公開稱讚,常用被動語態。也指以歌唱等讚美上帝。
hail	喝采,歡呼,把某人或某件事情推崇為英雄或傑作等,受詞後面常接as + 名詞(如as a hero, success等),較常用被動語態。另外也表示呼叫(計程車)。
commend	公開稱讚或認同某人或某件事情。常用被動語態。另外也表示託付或推薦(與recommend相似)。
compliment	稱讚,受詞時常是人。可以當動詞和名詞,當名詞時前面的動詞常用pay(如pay somebody compliments/ a compliment)。在語料庫中較多當名詞的用法。
acclaim	公開稱讚某人或某件事情,常用被動語態。在語料庫中較多當名詞的用法。
extol	正式用字。大力稱讚。

Unit 46 超越

StringNet語料庫出現次數

overtake	transcend	surpass	surmount
864	398	333	255

overtake（vi./vt.）

❖ 常用句型

S + overtake + O

❖ 例句

Do not overtake the vehicle in front of you on a mountain road.
在山區道路上不要超車。

Nuclear energy has overtaken oil as France's main fuel.
核電已經超越石油成為法國主要的燃料。

❖ 常用搭配詞

overtake the + n.
  number, UK, world, car.

adv. + overtake
  soon, suddenly, rapidly, gradually, finally, eventually, actually, illegally.

transcend（vt.）

❖ 常用句型

> **S + transcend + O**

❖ 例句

At the end of the story, the old man has transcended the fear of death.
在故事的結尾，這個老人已經超越對死亡的恐懼。

❖ 常用搭配詞

transcend the + n.

　　limitations, confines, world, limits, body, dichotomies, difference, status, barriers.

transcend + n.

　　differences, nature, reason, gender, greed, time, barriers, generations.

adv. + transcend

　　eventually.

surpass（vt.）

❖ 常用句型

> **S + surpass + O**

❖ 例句

China has surpassed the US as the world's largest retail market.
中國已經超越美國成為全世界最大的零售市場。

His performance tonight has surpassed my expectations.
他今晚的表演超越我的預期。

❖ 常用搭配詞

surpass +（det.） n.

anything, it, himself, them, attainment, Japan, expectations, beauty, China.

adv. + surpass

far, even, easily, comfortably, finally, rarely, quickly, greatly.

surmount（vt.）

❖ 常用句型

> **S + surmount + O**

❖ 例句

Although he survived the fire, he had to surmount his handicap.
雖然他在這場大火中存活下來，他必須克服他的肢體障礙。
The column is surmounted by a lion sculpture.
這根柱子頂端有一隻獅子的雕像。

❖ 常用搭配詞

surmount the + _n._
  barrier, crises.

_n._ + surmounted by
  construction, tower, building, column, foliage.

綜合整理

overtake	超越移動中的交通工具或行進中的人，超越到他們前面。也表示比別人或別的事情更成功、更重要、或更先進。另外也表示突襲等意義，所以在語料庫中出現次數較多。
transcend	正式用字。超越某件事情的界線。
surpass	比別人或別的事情更好或更大。
surmount	正式用字，通常用被動語態。超越問題或困難，也表示在某個東西的頂端或上面。

Unit 47 拆除

StringNet語料庫出現次數

demolish	dismantle
996	680

demolish（vt.）

❖ 常用句型

> **S + demolish + O**

❖ 例句

The old houses are being demolished to make way for a new shopping center.
他們正在拆這些老房子來蓋一棟新的購物中心。

❖ 常用搭配詞

demolish the + _n._

　house, chapel, wall, church, store, building, opposition, commons, bungalow.

adv. + demolish

　recently, completely, totally, partially, finally, largely, effectively, systematically, eventually, simply, quickly, deliberately, partly, hastily, subsequently.

dismantle（vt.）

❖ 常用句型

> **S + dismantle + O**

❖ 例句

He taught his son how to dismantle and assemble a gun.
他教他的兒子如何拆解和組合槍枝。

The new President planned to dismantle the healthcare system erected by the former President.
這新任總統打算要廢除前任總統建立的健保制度。

❖ 常用搭配詞

dismantle +（det.）n.
  power, system, provisions, valve, link, corporation, machine, plant.

adv. + dismantle
  completely, partly, subsequently, effectively, partially, immediately, carefully, single-handedly, ruthlessly, systematically.

綜合整理

demolish	將建築物拆除，也表示推翻某個說法。
dismantle	將機器或裝備的零件拆解，也表示逐漸廢除某個制度或組織。另外也有破壞等其他意義。

Unit 48 撤退，撤回，撤銷

StringNet語料庫出現次數

withdraw	retreat	revoke	repeal	rescind
4609	897	334	325	194

withdraw（vi./vt.）

❖ 常用句型

> **S + withdraw + O**

❖ 例句

He decided to withdraw his resignation.
他決定要撤銷辭職。

She withdrew from the beauty contest after the scandal.
她在這件醜聞之後退出選美比賽。

❖ 常用搭配詞

withdraw from the + _n._

contest, market, engagement, coalition, trial, world, contract, case, race, area, scheme, talks, deal, competition, business, country, UK, transaction, gulf, territory, project, Warsaw, arrangement, organization, squad, community, provision, university, commune, society, election, discussions, continent, agreement, region, commission, bidding, forest, purchase, agenda, proceedings.

withdraw one's + _n._

support, hand, troops, forces, labor, offer, objections, children, money, sponsorship, threat, remarks, consent, arm, candidature, nomination, candidacy, bid, proposal, head, claim, application, resignation, finger, allegation, opposition, backing, request, grant, plans, deposits, candidates, team, funding, appeal, business, approval, products, petition, assent, favor, insistence, comments, notice, concession, promise, interest, gaze, mind, savings.

adv. + withdraw

eventually, subsequently, formally, immediately, soon, actually, finally, suddenly, temporarily, gradually, quickly, progressively, quietly, simply, slowly, increasingly, voluntarily, officially, recently, promptly, abruptly, effectively, hastily, completely, steadily, slightly, largely, persistently, discreetly, instantly, ultimately, unexpectedly, prudently, gently, shortly, tactfully.

retreat（vi.）

❖ 常用句型

S + retreat（+ prep. + N）

❖ 例句

Government has retreated from the promise of full employment.
政府已經撤銷零失業率的承諾。
The troops retreated to their second line of defence.
那些軍隊撤退到他們的第二道防線。

❖ 常用搭配詞

retreat to the + <u>n.</u>

   bedroom, mountains, safety, towns, kitchen, edge, shade, country, river.

retreat from the + <u>n.</u>

   square, idea, promise, battle, market, city, field, policy, position.

retreat + <u>adv.</u>

   further, again, rapidly, hastily, gradually, swiftly, northwards, steadily.

revoke（vt.）

❖ 常用句型

> **S + revoke + O**

❖ 例句

His driving license was revoked for drunk driving.
他因為酒駕被撤銷駕照。

❖ 常用搭配詞

revoke +（det.）<u>n.</u>

   license, order, decision, permission, directions, recognition.

<u>adv.</u> + revoke

   formally, hereby.

repeal（vt.）

❖ 常用句型

> **S + repeal + O**

❖ 例句

The government repealed the ban on women flying combat aircraft.
政府撤銷不准女性駕駛戰機的禁令。

❖ 常用搭配詞

n. + be repealed
  act, legislation, laws.

repeal the + n.
  law, act, increase, requirement, legislation, ban.

adv. + repeal
  recently, immediately, impliedly, entirely.

rescind（vt.）

❖ 常用句型

> **S + rescind + O**

❖ 例句

The committee decided to rescind the nomination of the song as Best Original Song.
委員會決定撤銷提名這首歌為最佳原創歌曲。

❖ 常用搭配詞

rescind the + n.

contract, sale, agreement, order, notice, ban, declaration, bankruptcy.

adv. + rescind

formally.

綜合整理

withdraw	退出已經參加的活動或組織，也表示撤回已經提出或給予的支持、金錢、要求、言論等。
retreat	因為戰敗而撤兵，或因為太困難而撤銷原本的計畫。另外也表示後退遠離某人事物，或退到安靜或安全的地方。也可以當名詞表示引退處或宗教退修會。
revoke	正式使某個法律、協議、或決定失效。
repeal	政府撤銷某個法律。
rescind	正式廢除某個法律、協議、或決定。

Unit 49 沉沒，沉浸

StringNet語料庫出現次數

sink	immerse	submerge
3030	359	272

sink（vi./vt.）

❖ 常用句型

S + sink（+ O）

❖ 例句

The damaged boat sank to the bottom of the lake.

那艘破損的船沉到湖底。

❖ 常用搭配詞

sink + adv.

　in, down, back, deep, slowly, further, rapidly, quickly, below, immediately, wearily, gradually, slightly, overnight.

n.（s）+ sink

　heart, words, head, spirits, voice, boat, sun, ships, finger, body, shaft, water, hands, Titanic, chin, man, Ruth（人名）, eyes, aircraft, achievement, submarine, sand, guns, cross, rates.

sink a + n.
    ship, shaft, well.

immerse（vi./vt.）

❖ 常用句型

S + immerse（+ O）

❖ 例句

If you scald or burn yourself , immediately immerse the affected part in cold water for as long as possible.

如果你被燙傷或燒傷，立刻把傷處浸泡在水中愈久愈好。

❖ 常用搭配詞

immersed in the + n.
    water, detail, music, work.

adv. + immersed
    deeply, totally, completely, fully, half, partially.

submerge（vt.）

❖ 常用句型

> **S + submerge + O**

❖ 例句

Humans become unconscious after being submerged for 3 hours in water at 15°C.

人類如果泡在攝氏15度的水中超過三小時就會失去意識。

❖ 常用搭配詞

<u>n.（s）</u> + be submerged

  entrance, identify, question, body.

<u>n.</u> + submerged

  lies, bodies, stones.

<u>adv.</u> + submerged

  completely, totally, partially, partly, largely.

綜合整理

sink	沒入水面之下或向下沉，也表示心情下沉或物體、聲音等降低。當及物動詞時表示使沉沒。
immerse	完全沉入，浸泡，受詞可以是人或物。另外也表示人沉迷或陷入某事物。
submerge	以水或液體完全覆蓋。另外也表示隱藏或壓抑情感、意見等。

Unit 50 償還

StringNet語料庫出現次數

repayment	refund	reimbursement
1133	234	157

repayment（n.）

❖ 例句

Nancy has been keeping a tight budget in order to keep up repayment on a loan.

Nancy 用錢一直很省，為了要償還她的貸款。

❖ 常用搭配詞

adj. + repayment

  monthly, principal, weekly, regular, provisional, net, higher.

n. + repayment

  debt, mortgage, capital, loan, interest, tax, part, purchase.

repayment + n.

  period, mortgage, supplement, terms, schedule, loans, claim, methods, arrangements, date, obligations, table, system, examples, source, problems, level, conditions, proposals, program.

v. + repayment

claim, demand, meet, collect, obtain, calculate, make, seek, extend, negotiate.

refund（n.）

❖ 例句

Ticket refunds can be collected from the Opera House booking office.
觀眾可以在歌劇院的售票處辦理退票。
No refund will be made without a valid receipt.
沒有有效的收據就不能辦理退費。

❖ 常用搭配詞

n. + refund

tax, cash, ticket, vat, money, export, pounds.

adj. + refund

full, all.

v. + a refund

get, claim, have, refuse, obtain, make, give, demand, receive, like.

reimbursement（n.）

❖ 例句

You will receive reimbursement for any additional costs incurred in working abroad.

你在國外工作時所需要的任何額外的開銷都可以報帳（銷帳）。

❖ 常用搭配詞

v. + reimbursement

  receive, claim, seek.

adj. + reimbursement

  prospective, retrospective, partial, general.

reimbursement + n.

  systems, schemes, record.

綜合整理

repayment	不可數名詞。償還，尤其是抵押貸款等的還款。
refund	可數名詞。因為退掉不滿意的商品或服務而得的退款。
reimbursement	正式用字，把錢補償給先墊錢或付錢的人，也就是銷帳。也表示賠償損失的錢。

Unit 51 承認

StringNet語料庫出現次數

admit	recognize	acknowledge	concede	confess
10911	5811	4167	1774	1564

admit（vi./vt.）

❖ 常用句型

> S + admit +（to somebody）+（that）子句
> S + admit（to）Ving
> S + admit + O

❖ 例句

I must admit I am hungry.
我必須承認我很餓。

The candidate admitted to having accepted some improper contributions.
這位候選人承認收受了一些不當的獻金。

He refused to admit defeat.
他拒絕認輸。

❖ 常用搭配詞

the _n.（s）_ + admit

　government, company, department, minister, plaintiff, commission.

admit to having + Vpp

had, done, raped, felt.

adv. + admit

freely, later, readily, finally, openly, actually, publicly, cheerfully, frankly, recently, grudgingly, privately, eventually, candy, officially, immediately, generally, informally, effectively, reluctantly, newly, allegedly, previously, rarely, sadly, virtually, subsequently, certainly, reportedly, honestly, normally, tacitly, explicitly, easily, simply, necessarily, repeatedly, modestly, shyly, randomly, apparently, willingly, unashamedly, sheepishly.

recognize（vt.）

❖ 常用句型

> S + recognize + O（as + N）
> S + recognize +（that）子句

❖ 例句

The US did not recognize the legitimacy of the present government in this region.
美國不承認這區域目前政府的合法性。
Many scientists do not recognize the existence of ghosts.
許多科學家不承認鬼的存在。

❖ 常用搭配詞

adv. + recognize

widely, generally, immediately, officially, formally, internationally, clearly, explicitly, increasingly, fully, universally, actually, legally, instantly, publicly, finally, implicitly, readily, nationally, frankly, socially, gradually, simply, rightly, effectively, commonly, normally, eventually.

acknowledge（vt.）

❖ 常用句型

> S + acknowledge + O（as + N）
> S + acknowledge + that 子句

❖ 例句

He is widely acknowledged as the spiritual leader of environmentalists.
他被公認為環保人士的精神領袖。
He acknowledged that he couldn't have made the film without his father's support.
他承認若是沒有他父親的支持他無法拍攝這部電影。

❖ 常用搭配詞

（det.）n.（s）+ acknowledge that

government, committee, state, people, company, report, minister, paper, group, rangers, employers, bank, gentleman, tenant, shipowner, authors, purchaser.

acknowledge the + n.

need, importance, existence, fact, extent, applause, support, role, truth, authority, possibility, value, significance, help, work contribution, source, problem, order, government, superiority, assistance, difficulty, right, end, reality, impact, success, receipt, power, debt, distinction, point, interest, validity, failure, hit, strength, justice, lack, relevance, sovereignty, lack difference, danger, progress, nature, ability, slaughter, king, necessity, inevitability.

adv. + acknowledge

widely, generally, readily, gratefully, publicly, openly, universally, fully, officially, barely, formally, hereby, finally, simply, implicitly, explicitly, freely, rarely, tacitly, actually, clearly, kindly, duly, sufficiently, merely, effectively, generously, quickly, briefly, subsequently, increasingly, gladly, certainly, privately, proudly, adequately, recently, greatly, justly, accurately, repeatedly, frankly, gravely, happily, warmly.

concede（vi./vt.）

❖ 常用句型

> **S + concede +（that）子句**

❖ 例句

He finally conceded that it was the only possible solution.
他終於承認那是唯一的解決之道。

❖ 常用搭配詞

（det.） n.（s） + conceded that
   government, association, advisers, UK.

concede the + n.
   principle, right, possibility, championship, importance, impossibility, truth.

confess（vi./vt.）

❖ 常用句型

S + confess to（doing）something
S + confess +（that）子句
S + confess + O

❖ 例句

She confessed to having been a spy for 12 years.
她承認她做了十二年的間諜。

He confessed that he was not a good father.
他承認自己不是一個好父親。

The bible says if we confess our sins to God, he will forgive us.
聖經上說如果我們向上帝認罪，祂會饒恕我們。

❖ 常用搭配詞

（det.） n. (s) + confess

Maggie（人名）, people, woman, man, girl, patient.

 adv. + confess

well, only.

confess one's + n.

sins, name, failure, love, need, ignorance, doubts, desire.

綜合整理

admit	勉強承認某件事情是真實的或某人是對的，也表示承認自己的錯誤，尤其是犯案。
recognize	承認某個政府、機構、或文件的合法性或權威性，也表示接受某件事情是真實的，可以用在被動語態表示某事物的重要性或美好被眾人所公認。另外也表示認出。
acknowledge	承認某件事情是真實的，某個（不好的）狀況真實存在，某事物的重要性或美好，以及某人的權威性。另外也表示答謝、注意等多種意義。
concede	不得不承認某件事情是真實的或正確的，即使自己希望那不是真的，在競賽中認輸（相當於admit defeat）。另外也表示退讓。
confess	認罪，尤其是向警方、神父、上帝等，也表示承認自己的弱點或尷尬的情形。

Unit 52 懲罰

StringNet語料庫出現次數

penalty	punishment
3378	2447

penalty（n.）

❖ 例句

The existence of death penalty has been a controversial issue in our country.
在我們的國家，死刑的存廢一直是個具爭議性的話題。

❖ 常用搭配詞

adj. + penalty

maximum, financial, three, fixed, severe, heavy, second, criminal, late, stiffer, mandatory, third, disputed, new, tough, legal, non-custodial, harsher, appropriate, dubious, same, controversial, early, serious, automatic, simple, dramatic, last-minute, resulting, short, missed, potential, higher, extreme, obvious, crowded, ultimate, top.

punishment（n.）

❖ 例句

Corporal punishment has been abolished in many countries.
許多國家都已經禁止體罰。

❖ 常用搭配詞

adj. + punishment

corporal, capital, physical, severe, appropriate, sufficient, terrible, maximum, same, real, heavy, eternal, suitable, harsh, criminal, worst, collective, excessive, divine, subsequent, legal, public, credible, unusual, immediate, retributive, effective, unfair, dreadful, self-inflicted, reasonable, judicial, inevitable, social, due, double, cruel, deserving, determining, temporary, statutory, serious.

綜合整理

penalty	因為違反法律、規範、或協議而受到的懲罰，包含罰鍰，也表示做壞事的報應。另外也表示做某件事情必須付的代價，以及球賽的罰球。
punishment	處罰的罰則或行為。

Unit 53 事件

StringNet語料庫出現次數

matter	event	affair	occasion	incident	episode	occurrence
26011	20577	10372	8930	5131	2064	1342

matter（n.）

❖ 例句

I tried to explain to them, but it only made matters worse.
我試著向他們解釋，卻讓事情變得更糟。
It's only a matter of time before he left the band.
他遲早會離開這個樂團的。

❖ 常用搭配詞

adj. + matter

another, different, important, simple, serious, financial, sexual, personal, whole, certain, legal, small, environmental, easy, technical, political, practical, commercial, economic, laughing, related, private, criminal, relevant, religious, administrative, minor, complex, following, procedural, urgent, social, trivial, internal, delicate, domestic, military, civil, controversial, disciplinary, complicated, mundane, professional, cultural, medical, suspended, spiritual, sensitive, general, educational, public, crucial, individual, confidential, local, foreign, empirical, everyday, basic, separate, ordinary, secular, ethical, intimate, moral, regulatory, significant.

event（n.）

❖ 例句

The Olympic Games is a major sporting event in the world.
奧運是全世界重大的體育盛事。
The Arab Spring is one of the top 9 political events of 2011.
阿拉伯之春是2011年九大政治事件的其中之一。

❖ 常用搭配詞

adj. + event

special, social, major, recent, annual, historical, political, unlikely, future, international, subsequent, mental, significant, external, rare, certain, fund-raising, sponsored, single, local, dramatic, forthcoming, actual, whole, natural, current, public, final, cultural, key, physical, popular, strange, traumatic, real, specified, momentous, later, individual, different, specific, next, unique, three-day, tragic, environmental, exciting, last, everyday, prestigious, contemporary, unusual, adverse, early, terrible, new, historic, neural, severe, regular, happy, communicative, musical, stressful, extraordinary, catastrophic, separate, unexpected, successful, evolutionary, contingent, educational, inaugural, interesting, related, latter, premier, probable, minor, following, crucial, top, common, recurrent, military, unforeseen, disturbing, previous, spectacular, several, organized, exceptional, competitive, running, critical, indoor.

affair（n.）

❖ 例句

He was still seen intermittently with the married woman after their love affair had been allegedly over.

據傳他們的戀情已告終止，但之後他仍然偶爾被人目睹與那位有夫之婦在一起，

Foreign affairs are not often an important factor in British general elections.

外交事務在英國大選中不常是一個重要的因素。

❖ 常用搭配詞

adj. + affairs

foreign, internal, social, current, public, economic, international, external, financial, religious, political, domestic, corporate, rural, human, cultural, legal, military, European, Scottish, local, regional, personal, Indian, environmental, administrative, practical, municipal, civil, everyday.

n. + affair

love, family, Westland, Guinness, recruit, spycatcher, watergate, maxwell, office.

occasion（n.）

❖ 例句

I have seen him drunk on several occasions.

有幾次我看到他喝醉了。

It is normal in this country to hug strangers on happy occasions.
在這個國家，在快樂的場合擁抱陌生人是正常的。

❖ 常用搭配詞

adj. + occasion

several, many, special, another, rare, previous, few, numerous, social, different, last, separate, great, odd, ceremonial, important, memorable, certain, earlier, same, five, future, later, happy, public, royal, formal, subsequent, given, recent, momentous, frequent, sporting, joyous, countless, famous, possible, historic, single, festive, sad, enjoyable, wonderful, successive, whole.

incident（n.）

❖ 例句

Two men died last night in a shooting incident.
昨晚有兩個男子在一場槍擊事件中喪生。

The criticism cannot be justified if it is based on one isolated incident.
如果這個批判是基於單一獨立事件，那麼它就沒有道理。

❖ 常用搭配詞

adj. + incident

this, such, similar, violent, serious, separate, isolated, whole, major, particular, latest, alleged, recent, unfortunate, worst, many, second, earlier, embarrassing, several, small, single, diplomatic, amusing, reported, off-the-ball, ugly, following, unpleasant, each, dramatic, specific, regrettable, tragic, international, nuclear, numerous, bizarre, mysterious, terrible, trivial, stabbing, famous, unsavory, strange, curious.

episode（n.）

❖ 例句

He wishes he could erase the whole humiliating episode from his memory.
他希望能把這件丟臉的事件從他的記憶中消除。
He has been readmitted to hospital following a psychotic episode.
最近他因為又有精神異常的事故而再次住院。

❖ 常用搭配詞

adj. + episode

  this, whole, entire, particular, single, bleeding, psychotic, unfortunate, recent, traumatic, remarkable, previous, unpleasant, early, odd, embarrassing.

occurrence（n.）

❖ 例句

This is a comparatively rare occurrence, but it certainly does occur.
這種事情很罕見，但是它確實會發生。
Suicide and self-injury is an everyday occurrence in prison.
自殺和自殘在監獄是每天都會發生的事情。

❖ 常用搭配詞

<u>adj.</u> + occurrence

common, rare, frequent, regular, everyday, each, widespread, daily, first, unusual, occasional, familiar, actuar, annual, natural, single, unlikely, seasonal, global, identical, repeated, sporadic.

綜合整理

matter	必須考慮或處理的事件，例如一個主題或狀況（如personal matter個人私事），常用在正式文章。另外也表示物質，因此在語料庫出現的次數很多。
event	重要、有趣、或是不尋常的事件，另外也指許多人一起參加的大型活動，例如派對、運動賽事、抗議等（如fund-raising event募款活動，annual event一年舉辦一次的活動）。
affair	人所做或是經歷的一個事件或一連串相關的事件（如foreign affairs外交事務），尤其是引起大眾注意或震驚的（the watergate affair水門事件）。單數affair常用來表示男女戀愛事件，尤其是婚外情。複數名詞前面也時常出現國家或地區的形容詞（如Korean affairs）表示有關該國的外交事務。
occasion	事情發生的時間、場合，或是重大社交活動或儀式。另外也指做某件事情的適當時機（如 an occasion for celebration 該慶祝的時候）。
incident	重要、不尋常、或是暴力的單一事件，有負面意義，前面常接負面意義的形容詞（如tragic, unfortunate, violent等）。常用在新聞報導的正式用字。
episode	一段短時間內發生的事情a least-known episode in the history（一段很少人知道的歷史事件）。另外也指電視連續劇的一集。
occurrence	發生的事情，前面時常皆表示頻率的形容詞（如frequent頻繁的，sporadic零星的）。動詞是occur（發生）。

Unit 54 善變的，多變的

StringNet語料庫出現次數

variable	unstable	unpredictable	inconsistent	erratic	fickle
1305	692	665	635	392	121

variable（adj.）

❖ 例句

The sponge toy is highly variable in shape.

這個海綿玩具的形狀可以做各種變化。

The saw has a 550watt motor and features variable speed.

這個鋸子有550瓦的馬達而且可以變速。

❖ 常用搭配詞

variable + n.

analysis, costs, speed, rate, quality, length, loop, information, factors, results, number, degrees, amounts, standards, name, proportions, ratio, rule, nature, time, component, pitch, temperature.

adv. + variable

highly, very, more, extremely, infinitely, continuously, slightly, rather, quite, widely, increasingly.

unstable（adj.）

❖ 例句

He decided not to go to the country because of its unstable political situation.
他決定不去那個國家，因為那裏的政治不安定。

❖ 常用搭配詞

unstable + _n._

　　angina, manifold, condition, region, situation, state, ground, government,
　　demand, environment, world, period, mineral, atom.

adv. + unstable

　　very, highly, mentally, emotionally, inherently, rather, increasingly, relatively,
　　notoriously, politically, slightly, thermally, dangerously, geographically.

unpredictable（adj.）

❖ 例句

The winds in the valley are unpredictable and sometimes dangerously strong.
山谷裡的風變化不定，有時強到很危險的地步。

❖ 常用搭配詞

unpredictable + n.

　component, nature, ways, results, weather, movement, business, behavior, changes, fashion, times, man, consequences, personality, timing, reactions, creatures, variables, manner, process.

adv. + unpredictable

　more, totally, highly, increasingly, notoriously, somewhat, completely, essentially, rather.

inconsistent（adj.）

❖ 例句

The tennis player's performance has been highly inconsistent in the past yer.
這名籃球選手的表現在過去一年相當不穩定。

❖ 常用搭配詞

inconsistent + n.

　results, state, way, consequences, season.

adv. + inconsistent

　totally, quite, somewhat, highly, rather, wholly.

erratic（adj.）

❖ 例句

The patient struggled to control his erratic breathing.
這病人掙扎地控制他不規律的呼吸。

❖ 常用搭配詞

erratic + n.

course, performance, investment, nature, career, rainfall, beat, season, supply, movements, mood.

❖ 常用搭配詞

adv. + erratic

more, very, somewhat, less, increasingly, rather, wildly, slightly.

fickle（adj.）

❖ 例句

Fame is like a fickle mistress.
名聲就像一個善變的女人。

❖ 常用搭配詞

fickle + n.

finger, world, game, fashion, weather, creatures, friends, lover, mistress, wind.

adv. + fickle

notoriously, very, most, more.

綜合整理

variable	有可能會改變的，時好時壞的，或可以調整改變的。時常用來形容速率、長度、成分等。
unstable	事物有可能突然改變，尤其是變得更糟糕，後面的名詞可能是病情或政治情勢等，很少是人。也指人的性情善變以至於無法預知他的行為或反應。
unpredictable	一直在變化中以至於無法預測接下來會發生甚麼事情。
inconsistent	不穩定的，表示人的行為或作品時常由好轉壞。較常表示不一致的、矛盾的。
erratic	不規律的，反覆無常的人事物，另外也表示乖僻、古怪的。
fickle	對人事物的喜好變化不定，不可靠，有負面意義。

另外mercurial是文學用字，形容人的情感或脾氣善變，因為在語料庫出現次數少，因此在此沒討論。

Unit 55 呻吟

StringNet語料庫出現次數

moan	groan	wail	howl
793	782	412	381

moan（vi.）

❖ 常用句型

> **S + moan（+ prep. +N）**

❖ 例句

The patient moaned in pain.

那位病人因為疼痛而呻吟。

I could hear the wind moaning through the window.

我可以聽見嗚咽的風聲穿越窗戶。

❖ 常用搭配詞

n.（s） + moan

  wind, people, Ruth（人名）, man.

moan + adv.

  softly, quietly, loudly, aloud, gently, faintly, hoarsely, helplessly.

groan（vi.）

❖ 常用句型

> **S + groan（+ prep. +N）**

❖ 例句

He groaned and put his head in his hands.
他發出呻吟然後把頭埋入雙手中。

❖ 常用搭配詞

groan + adv.
　inwardly, softly, loudly, quietly, miserably, heavily, silently.

wail（vi.）

❖ 常用句型

> **S +wail（+ prep. +N）**

❖ 例句

"What are we going to do ?" she wailed tearfully.
她含著眼淚哀叫著說：「那我們要怎麼辦？」
The siren of the red fire engine wailed and faded into the sounds of general traffic.
紅色消防車的警報聲響起，然後逐漸消失在車水馬龍聲中。

❖ 常用搭配詞

n. (s) + wail (ed)

she, he, sirens, woman, voice, Robyn（人名）, wind, music.

wailed + adv.

helplessly.

howl（vi.）

❖ 常用句型

> **S +howl（+ prep. +N）**

❖ 例句

The strong wind howled about the house, driving rain against the windows.
狂風在房子四周淒厲嚎叫，雨水被風吹打在窗戶上。

❖ 常用搭配詞

n. (s) + howl

wind, dogs, Jackals, soul, dive-bomb, siren.

howl + adv.

outside, round, mournfully, appallingly, uncontrollably.

綜合整理

moan	因為疼痛、不快樂、或性高潮而發出低沉持續的呻吟，和groan相似。在語料庫中大多是負面意義，也指低沉的風聲。
groan	因為疼痛、挫折、失望、或享受而發出低沉持續的呻吟，主詞通常是人，在語料庫中大多是負面意義。和moan相似。
wail	大聲哭叫或哀叫，語料庫中的主詞是人或警報聲。另外也表示放聲大哭。
howl	因為不高興、生氣、憤怒、或疼痛而哭嚎，或者因為興奮開心而發出持續而大聲的喊叫。另外也表示狼、狗等動物的長聲嚎叫。在語料庫中主詞通常不是人，而是風聲、動物、或警報聲等。

Unit 56 商品

StringNet語料庫出現次數

goods	commodity	merchandise
10044	1497	239

goods（n.）

❖ 例句

The significant increase in the number of heavy goods vehicles was not foreseen when the highways were designed.

當設計這些高速公路的時候並沒有先預知重型貨車的數量會大幅增加。

It is clear from the table that during the past ten years exports of goods and services have grown 11 percent each year on average.

從這張表格可以清楚看出在過去十年商品和服務的出口平均每年成長百分之十一。

❖ 常用搭配詞

n. + goods

consumer, household, capital, leather, cotton, sports, trade, export, railway, leisure, metal, tobacco, manufacturing, farm, merit, paper, engineering, dairy, Christmas, electronics, silk, transport.

adj. + goods

manufactured, stolen, heavy, public, electrical, industrial, luxury, imported, British, agricultural, unascertained, finished, defective, cultural, foreign, perishable, final, worldly, private, dangerous, dry, faulty, second-hand, electronic, primary, durable, western, home-produced, woolen, domestic, essential, unmixed, unsolicited, branded, symbolic, counterfeit, cheap, shoddy, commercial, packaged, expensive, damaged, physical, duty-free, unsold, scarce, fake, mass-produced, Japanese, mixed, daily.

commodity（n.）

❖ 例句

The fall in commodity prices means that Third World countries must produce more to earn the same amount.

物價下跌的意義是第三世界必須提高產量才可以賺到同樣多的錢。

❖ 常用搭配詞

commodity + n.

prices, production, markets, futures, economy, exchange, trading, form, chemicals, arbitrations, brokers, traders, exports, business, loan, system, circulation, producers, exporters, taxes, item, products, support, sector, producer, developments, anarchy.

adj. + commodity

valuable, basic, rare, scarce, primary, agricultural, precious, petty, international, capitalist, saleable, expensive, main, perishable, marketable, industrial, cheap, taxed, essential, various, final, real, non-fuel, major, private, raw, alienable, luxury, global, profitable.

merchandise（n.）

❖ 例句

Frequently catalogues are supplied giving a range of merchandise for customers to choose from.

含有包含各種商品的目錄會經常提供給顧客挑選。

The college shop sells a wide range of merchandise form sweatshirts to teddy-bears.

這間大學商店賣很多商品，從汗衫到泰迪熊都有。

❖ 常用搭配詞

merchandise + n.

　　trade, imports, exports, catalogue, promotion.

adj. + merchandise

　　other, general, important, same.

綜合整理

goods	複數名詞。製造好以供銷售的成品。在英式英文中指被火車等運送的貨物。前面的形容詞或名詞時常表示商品的種類（agricultural goods農產品）、材質（cotton goods棉製品）、性質（perishable goods易腐壞商品）、或狀況（damaged goods受損商品）等。
commodity	可數名詞。可以買賣的產品。前面不常接名詞，後面常接和商品買賣有關的名詞（如commodity prices物價、commodity circulation物流、commodity market商品市場、commodity exporters出口商等）。
merchandise	正式用字。不可數名詞。已經上架正在銷售的商品（如merchandise catalogue商品目錄，merchandise promotion商品促銷）。

Unit 57 生產，製造

StringNet語料庫出現次數

produce	manufacture
30025	1392

produce（vt.）

❖ 常用句型

> **S + produce + O**

❖ 例句

This factory produced cheap goods to be sold to Mainland China.
那間工廠生產便宜的商品以銷售到中國大陸。

Photosynthesis produces oxygen.
光合作用會產生氧氣。

❖ 常用搭配詞

n. + produced by

figures, effect, report, output, work, paper, items, corrosion, waste, information, document, services, products, changes, toxins, patterns, ammonia, inhibition, conditions, goods, results, chemicals, sound, field, leaflet, oxygen, material, pressure, publication, file, enegry, results, literature, compounds, symptoms, text, map, breakage, list, current, evidence, wine, surplus, milk, electricity, ambiguity, ranking, fluid, methane, force, picture, rate, print, explosion, image crisis, diarrhea, tension, liquid.

<u>n. (s)</u> + produce

order, ability, company, work, system, effect, material, capacity, services, failure, figures, power, mass, people, data, goods, industry, energy, information, government, items, report, farm, attempt, oil, output, plant, water, need, waste, cells, conditions, garden, works, manufacturers, way, papers, labor, pressure, gas, team, group, factory, engine, method, body, process, changes, wine, techniques, species, materials, products, chemicals, war, resources, reports, effects, evidence, man, farmers, children, research, series, commodities, economy, sound, business, Britain, results, texts, coal, files, society, country, fact, heat, land, corrosion, patterns, school, men, model, images, committee, food, computer, acid, plutonium, organisms, opportunity, idea, world, talks, workers, question, motor, software, electricity, neutrons, females, desire, tendency, dioxide, publishers, technology, eggs, forest, animal, enterprises, grapes, air, cars, printer, movements, design.

manufacture（vt.）

❖ 常用句型

> **S + manufacture + O**

❖ 例句

All the early supplies of penicillin which came to the public were manufactured in America.
早期大眾買到的盤尼西林都是在美國製造的。

❖ 常用搭配詞

n. + manufactured by
　products, engines, equipment, stationery, easel.

manufacture the + n.
　product, videos, machines, things, oil, brands, article, wings, goods.

綜合整理

produce	意義範圍廣大，包含製造某個結果或效果，生產出可以供人使用或購買的東西，文字創作，懷孕生產，或自然界生產農作物等，常用被動語態。另外也當名詞表示農產品。
manufacture	用機器大量生產商品或材料，常用被動語態。另外也指虛構。和fabricate相似。

Unit 58 容忍

StringNet語料庫出現次數

stand	bear	tolerate	endure
30762	16949	1149	1074

stand（vt.）

❖ 常用句型

> S + stand + O

❖ 例句

She couldn't stand the noise of children.
她不能忍受孩子們的噪音。

❖ 常用搭配詞

stand the + <u>n.</u>

  pace, strain, people, test, pain, sight, temperature, nonsense, heat, risk.

bear（vt.）

❖ 常用句型

> S + bear + O

❖ 例句

He couldn't bear the sight of his ex-wife.

他不願意再見到他的前妻。

Kindergartens were first to bear the brunt of low birth rate.

幼稚園首當其衝忍受少子化的衝擊。

❖ 常用搭配詞

bear the + n.

brunt, thought, cost, burden, weight, title, pain, loss, risk, idea, consequences, truth, sight, silence, cold, grief.

tolerate（vt.）

❖ 常用句型

> **S + tolerate + O**

❖ 例句

We will not tolerate any kind of bullying.

我們不會容忍任何形式的霸凌。

❖ 常用搭配詞

tolerate the + n.

presence, loss, idea, disturbance, heat.

endure（vt.）

❖ 常用句型

> **S + endure + N/ Ving**

❖ 例句

The cancer patient can no longer endure the pain.
這癌症病人再也無法忍受痛楚。

❖ 常用搭配詞

endure the + n.

  pain, thought, sight, indignity, smell, noise, ordeal.

綜合整理

stand	及物動詞。表示人忍耐、接受、應付困境，也表示物品能長時間承受某種情況而不會損壞。和tolerate相似。通常用在否定句或疑問句。另外常當作不及物動詞表示站立等多種意義，或名詞表示攤位等多種意義，所以在語料庫出現次數很多。
bear	及物動詞。勇敢地接受、忍耐困難、痛苦的環境。和stand相似。另外表示其他多種意義，也當名詞表示多種意義，所以在語料庫出現次數很多。
tolerate	及物動詞。容忍別人的行為、言語、或信念而不加以批評或懲罰，也表示容忍自己不喜歡的不愉快或困難的事情。
endure	及物動詞。長期忍受痛苦或困難而不抱怨。

Unit 59 容易，簡單的

StringNet語料庫出現次數

easy	simple	facile
19302	15626	104

easy（adj.）

❖ 例句

The English final test was very easy.
這次英文期末考很簡單。

❖ 常用搭配詞

easy + n.

access, way, reach, task, pronunciation, target, life, matter, job, money, answers, victory, part, question, win, solution, work, passage, decision, step, game, catch, process, identification, reading, opportunity, concept, method, maintenance, choice, shot, handling, success, business, travel, retrieval, word, road, recipe.

simple（adj.）

❖ 例句

He longs for the simple life in countryside.
他嚮往鄉村簡單的生活。

❖ 常用搭配詞

simple + n.

way, reason, matter, form, example, answer, fact, things, case, method, explanation, model, solution, task, statement, truth, system, process, level, words, language, test, rules, message, procedure, approach, idea, formula, device, job, design, instructions, life, type, man, exercise, guidelines, pattern, concept, techniques, network, reaction, meal, ideas, illustration, story, description, facts, version, experiment, account, definition, remedy, organisms, soul, plan, game, step, ceremony, logic, contract, problems, introduction, faith, folk.

facile（adj.）

❖ 例句

The mayor was criticized for his facile judgement on this social issue.
市長因為對這個社會議題粗糙的評斷而受到指責。

❖ 常用搭配詞

facile + n.

equation, answer, generalizations.

綜合整理

easy	不須費力太多就能做成。
simple	單純不複雜，不難了解或做成。
facile	表示言論等過於簡略粗糙而不夠周延。也是正式用字指太容易得到的成功或成就，但是後面必須接名詞。

Unit 60 融化，溶解

StringNet語料庫出現次數

dissolve	melt	fuse	thaw
1507	1390	426	191

dissolve（vi./vt.）

❖ 例句

She dissolved the sugar in lukewarm water.
她把糖放在溫水中溶解。

❖ 常用搭配詞

n.（s）+ dissolve

　salt, sugar, oxygen, mineral, pellets.

melt（vi./vt.）

❖ 常用句型

S + melt（+ O）

❖ 例句

She ate the ice cream cone before it melted.
她在霜淇淋融化前趕緊把它吃掉。

❖ 常用搭配詞

melt the + _n._

   butter, chocolate, jelly, margarine.

fuse （vi./vt.）

❖ 常用句型

> **S + fuse （+ O）**

❖ 例句

Gold fuses at 1,064 °C.
黃金的熔點是攝氏1,064度。

❖ 常用搭配詞

_n. （s）_ + fuse

   lights, protons, glass, heat, gold, neutrons.

thaw （vi./vt.）

❖ 例句

The animals waited until the snow thawed to leave their burrows.
動物們一直等到雪融化了才離開他們的洞穴。

❖ 常用搭配詞

n. （s） + thaw

snow, glaciers, lake, ponds.

綜合整理

dissolve	固體溶解在液體之中。在語料庫中的用法大多表示解散（團體機構）。
melt	固體（因為受熱）融化成液體。
fuse	把二個物品融合在一起。也是工業用語。表示金屬或石頭因為受熱熔化。
thaw	冰或雪融化成水，也表示冷凍食物解凍。

Unit 61 縱容、寵愛

StringNet語料庫出現次數

spoil	indulge	pamper
1411	985	154

spoil（vt.）

❖ 常用句型

> **S + spoil + O/ oneself**

❖ 例句

He has spoiled his only daughter。
他把他的獨生女寵壞了。
Let me spoil you on your birthday.
你生日的時候讓我好好寵愛你吧!

❖ 常用搭配詞

spoil + n. （人）
　　him, you, me, yourself, themselves, oneself, us.

be + adv. spoilt
　　thoroughly, often, clearly, completely, usually.

indulge（vt.）

❖ 常用句型

> **S + indulge + O/ oneself**

❖ 例句

In the lecture the speaker encouraged mothers not to indulge their child.

在演講中那位演講者鼓勵媽媽們不要寵溺她們的孩子。

You should indulge yourself once in a while.

你應該偶而寵愛自己一下。

❖ 常用搭配詞

indulge + n.（人）

himself, themselves, them, myself, yourself, herself, him, ourselves, me, you.

indulge + one's + n.

taste, passion, love, interest, self-pity, imagination, desire, curiosity.

pamper（vt.）

❖ 常用句型

> **S + pamper + O/ oneself**

❖ 例句

Grandparents tend to pamper their grandchildren.
祖父母常會寵溺他們的孫子女。
I have never seen animals so pampered like her dog.
我從來沒有見過動物像她的狗如此受寵。

❖ 常用搭配詞

adv. + pampered
  thoroughly.

pampered + n.
  woman, beauty, girls.

綜合整理

spoil	寵壞，慣壞，受詞是人（如Spare the rod and spoil the child.孩子不打不成器），時常用被動語態（如S + be spoilt for choice選擇太多而讓人眼花撩亂，不知如何選擇）。另外也指破壞某事物的樂趣或用處（和ruin相似），或食物腐壞，受詞是事或物。
indulge	縱容，讓人為所欲為，即使是對他們不好的事情，受詞是人，也表示放縱某人的慾望或喜好，此時受詞不是人。另外也當不及物動詞表示耽溺於某件不好的事情（indulge in self-pity沉溺於自憐）。
pamper	寵壞，慣壞，和spoil相似。

Unit 62 憎恨

StringNet語料庫出現次數

hate	loathe	detest	abhor
4700	332	234	115

hate（vt.）

❖ 常用句型

> S + hate + O
> S + hate + to do something/ Ving

❖ 例句

He hates his parents.
他恨他的父母。
I hate having to work with him.
我很討厭必須和他一起工作。
I hate to sound callous, but you brought this on yourself.
我不想說無情的話，可是你真的是自作自受。

❖ 常用搭配詞

hate + _n._

people, women, school, mail, shopping, crowds, jazz, children, animals, critics, opera, blacks, Christmas, cats, spiders, tea, exercise, untidiness, work, Sundays, England, books.

hate + Ving

having, going, doing, lying, making, seeing, talking, playing, living, getting, sitting, watching, driving, leaving, working, coming, saying, wearing, calling, cooking, waiting, taking, shopping, buying, sleeping, looking, writing, hurting, touching, eating, wasting, learning, speaking.

loathe（vt.）

❖ 常用句型

> **S + loathe + O/ Ving**

❖ 例句

Cathy was loathed by all her friends, who regarded her as a traitor.
Cathy所有的同學都痛恨她，是她為叛徒。
Even though he is a teacher, he loathed making public speeches.
縱然他是老師，他非常討厭在眾人面前發表演說。

❖ 常用搭配詞

loathe the + n.

idea, way, thought, man, metal, sight.

loathe + Ving

having, seeing, killing, losing.

loathe to + Vroot

leave, give, take, admit, see, accept.

detest（vt.）

❖ 常用句型

> **S + detest + O**

❖ 例句

She and her husband detest each other.
她和她的丈夫彼此憎恨。

❖ 常用搭配詞

detest + n.
　Picasso, modesty, religions, children.

detest the + n.
　architect, fact.

abhor（vt.）

❖ 常用句型

> **S + abhor + O**

❖ 例句

Most people abhor violence.
大部分的人憎惡暴力。

❖ 常用搭配詞

abhor + _n._

　idleness, deception, solitude.

abhor the + _n._

　idea, notion, criticism.

綜合整理

hate	憎恨某個人事物，通常帶有憤怒。後面可以接動名詞或不定詞。
loathe	痛恨某人或某事物，和detest相似。在字典上此字後面常接動名詞Ving，但是在語料庫此字後面較多接to do something（如loathe to leave）。
detest	痛恨某人或某事物。
abhor	正式用字，憎惡某種行為或思想，尤其是不道德的。

Unit 63 錯誤

StringNet語料庫出現次數

error	mistake	fault
5905	5156	4111

error（n.）

❖ 例句

It is basically a process of trial and error to find the cosmetics that will suit you best.

要找到最適合你的化妝品基本上是一個嘗試錯誤的過程。

The report of the investigation concluded that the air crash had been caused by human errors.

調查報告的結論是這場空難是因為人為疏失造成的。

❖ 常用搭配詞

adj. + errors

standard, human, random, factual, minor, grammatical, common, defensive, past, possible, small, large, refractive, basic, systematic, phonological, typographical, fundamental, serious, jurisdictional, gross, significant, occasional, expectational, technical, individual, inherent, uncorrelated, lexical, numerous, positional, major, political, genetic, apparent, transient, fatal, syntactic, silly, grave, severe, trivial, detected, potential, administrative, subsequent, previous, inevitable, reported.

n. + error

syntax, lifespan, position, measurement, pilot, computer, driver, sampling, spelling, prediction, equation, printing, category, timing, closure, 1%, arithmetic, documentation, selection.

mistake（n.）

❖ 例句

There are 12 spelling mistakes in your report.
你的報告中有12個拼字錯誤。
He made a mistake of choosing Henry as his partner.
他選擇Henry做他的合夥人是個錯誤。

❖ 常用搭配詞

adj. + mistake

big, same, terrible, great, serious, common, fatal, bad, first, expensive, dreadful, worst, major, costly, little, easy, grave, genuine, fundamental, deliberate, disastrous, elementary, silly, classic, ghastly, stupid, enormous, occasional, understandable, strategic, colossal, rare, tactical, political, tragic, basic, main, unfortunate, factual, small, tiny, huge, natural, original, innocent, awful, cognitive, profound, idiotic, slight, psychological, philosophical, embarrassing, alleged, minor, obvious, unilateral, unreasonable.

n. + mistake

spelling, police, government, management, policy, security.

fault（n.）

❖ 例句

It was all my fault.

這都是我的錯。

His injury was caused by the fault of a negligent motorist.

他的受傷是一位疏忽的汽車駕駛人造成的。

❖ 常用搭配詞

adj. + fault

own, any, electrical, common, serious, mechanical, technical, structural, major, minor, same, possible, stupid, inherent, individual, numerous, moral, obvious, silly, grievous, perceived, alleged, reported, great, human, lethal, occasional.

fault + n.

element, diagnosis, tolerance, finding, system, resilience, lies, repair.

綜合整理

error	行為、言論、知識、或是信念上無意的錯誤，這裡指的錯誤可能是不正確、不真實的、或是不符合大家所接受的行為規範。也指電腦的錯誤。和mistake相似。前面的形容詞時常是有關語言文法或數學計算。
mistake	行為、言論、或想法的錯誤，導致不好的後果。如錯誤判斷、粗心大意、或誤解。和error相似，但是有可能是故意犯的錯（如deliberate mistake刻意的錯誤，strategic mistake策略性犯錯等）。
fault	導致壞事發生的過錯，可能是因為犯錯或者沒做到某件事情。另外也指機械或設計上的缺點瑕疵或個人個性上的重大缺點。另外也表示地質學的斷層（如dangerous fault危險的斷層，而不是危險的錯誤）。

Unit 64 速度

StringNet語料庫出現次數

rate	speed	pace	velocity	tempo
30164	7764	3331	1043	442

rate（n.）

❖ 例句

Infant mortality rates are high in Africa and many children did not survive into adulthood.

非洲的嬰兒死亡率很高，而且很多兒童沒能活到長大成人。

❖ 常用搭配詞

<u>n.</u> + rate

exchange, interest, growth, inflation, unemployment, tax, wage, success, discount, heart, mortality, death, birth, response, crime, pulse, market, mortgage, recurrence, failure, bank, lending, divorce, fertility, accident, survival, strike, hit, pass, production, detection, suicide, mutation, conversion, error, rotation, relapse, drop-out, participation, infusion, turnover, refusal, savings, conviction, profit, replacement, casualty, attendance, transfer, occupancy, literacy, completion, usage, take-up, murder, stocking, reaction, learning, citation, dollar, target, vacancy, fatality, abstention, arrest, loan, recovery, marriage, reproduction, pregnancy, injury, abortion, acceptance, admission, sampling, respiration, deposit, withdrawal, arrival.

adj. + rate

high, basic, lower, annual, fixed, low, metabolic, average, flat, standard, top, reduced, current, cheap, expected, domestic, faster, natural, present, new, rapid, hourly, marginal, premium, constant, full, official, alarming, risk-free, slower, normal, increased, maximum, local, forward, fair, actual, minimum, poor, competitive, respiratory, central, overall, healing, floating, variable, national, daily, increasing, slow, commercial, long-term, concessionary, composite, steady, reasonable, good, future, general, given, annualized, initial, favorable, nominal, weekly, internal, appropriate, prevailing, old, net, discounted, male, preferential, gross, jobless, unprecedented, accelerating, modest, interbank, corresponding, critical, peeking, effective, relative, negative, ordinary, age-specific, offered, falling, proper, astonishing.

speed（n.）

❖ 例句

You'd better stick to the speed limit.
你最好遵守速限。
He is driving at the speed of 120 kph.
他正在以時速120公里開車。

❖ 常用搭配詞

adj. + speed

high, top, average, maximum, full, constant, low, variable, normal, slow, breakneck, forward, steady, increasing, greater, astonishing, running, incredible, increased, good, excessive, surprising, vertical, remarkable, reasonable, fixed, considerable, possible, amazing, correct, alarming, actual, sheer, superior, sufficient, reduced, rotational, frightening, mean, legal, limiting, uncanny, terrific, relative, optimum, utmost, impressive, natural, equal, bewildering, faster, conversational, safe, stalling.

pace（n.）

❖ 例句

They walked at a leisurely pace along the street.
他們沿著街道緩慢悠閒地走。

❖ 常用搭配詞

adj. + pace

slow, leisurely, gather, rapid, fast, steady, brick, great, furious, hectic, blistering, cracking, unhurried, moderate, increasing, medium, accelerating, normal, frantic, excessive, easy, good, overall, sheer, right, quickening, relaxed, sinking, reasonable, present, sedate, breakneck, funereal, considerable, real, lively, frenetic, dramatic, varying, measured, gentle, gradual, plodding, uneven, relentless, running, tremendous, natural, narrative, suicidal, languorous, dynamic, quick.

n. + pace

walking, lightning, medium, training, gathering, race, recovery, record.

velocity（n.）

❖ 例句

The pattern of velocity of eye movements of REM sleep is quite unlike that of waking eye movements

睡眠中快速動眼期的眼球轉動速度模式和清醒時候的眼球轉動相當不一樣。

❖ 常用搭配詞

adj. + velocities

high, different, hypersonic, low, random, initial, sideways, peculiar, relative.

velocity of + n.

light, circulation, propagation, movement, sound.

n. + velocity

height, wave, wind, propagation, growth, fluid, shale, rotor, income, fall, phase, head, sedimentation, interval, electron, shock, motor, pulsar, impact, eye, outflow, transactions, water, deposition, peak, flow, coordinate, progression.

velocity + n.

profile, fluctuations, gradient, component, field, distribution, dispersion, measurement, range, scale, deficit, limitations, vector.

tempo（n.）

❖ 例句

She practiced the nocturne from memory with a metronome set at a very slow tempo.

她用背譜的方式練習那首小夜曲，同時把節拍器調到很慢的速度。

The tempo of his life quickened after he returned to work from vacation.

當他休假結束回去工作時，他的生活步調變得快速。

❖ 常用搭配詞

adj. + tempo

slow, faster, right, different, increasing, strict, same, own, headlong, moderate, original, quick.

n. + of tempo

changes, range, list, fluctuations.

綜合整理

rate	某件事情或某件事情的案例在一段時間之內發生的次數（如divorce rate離婚率）。也指某件事情發生的速度（如1.5 cm per year 一年多1.5公分）。
speed	某個東西移動的速度（如at a speed of 100 kph每小時100公里的速度）。也指某個行動或某件事情發生的速度（如high-speed train高速火車）。
pace	某件事情發生或完成的速度。也指走路、跑步、或移動的速度（如leisurely pace緩慢悠閒的速度）。
velocity	物理學上的速度（如the velocity of light光速）。
tempo	音樂上的速度、節拍。另外也指某件事情發生的速度。

Unit 65 騷動，動亂

StringNet語料庫出現次數

turmoil	agitation	turbulence	commotion
530	497	417	199

turmoil（n）

❖ 例句

The political turmoil in the country lasted for one year.

這個國家的政治動亂持續了一年。

She couldn't sleep because her mind was in turmoil.

她因為思緒混亂而無法入眠。

❖ 常用搭配詞

adj. + turmoil

political, inner, emotional, mental, ceaseless, constant, recent, economic, internal, religious, technological.

n.（s）+ be in turmoil

mind, heart, England, family.

agitation（n.）

❖ 例句

The region's agitation for autonomy is tearing the country apart.
這地區爭取自治的動亂正在使這個國家崩解中。
The police tried to talk to the kidnapper, who was in a state of agitation.
警方嘗試和激動焦躁的綁匪對話。

❖ 常用搭配詞

adj. + agitation

political, public, great, mass, growing, working-class, nationalist, joint, popular, pro-democracy, extreme, Hindu, inner, considerable, renewed, feminist, intense, gentle, widespread.

turbulence（n.）

❖ 例句

People in the region have suffered from political turbulence for many years.
此地區的人民多年來深受政治動亂之苦。

❖ 常用搭配詞

adj. + turbulence

political, isotropic, severe, wind-induced, considerable, financial, economic, bad, new, increasing, inner, slight, recent, emotional, social.

commotion（n.）

❖ 例句

Suddenly there was a commotion among the audience while he was lecturing.

當他在演講時觀眾席突然起了一陣騷動。

❖ 常用搭配詞

adj. + commotion

civil, sudden, great, slight, fearful, huge.

綜合整理

turmoil	不可數名詞。混亂、興奮、焦慮的狀態。常用在較大規模的動亂（如political turmoil政治動亂，economic turmoil經濟動亂）。
agitation	個人因為焦慮、緊張、不安而無法正常思考的狀態，或社會政治的抗爭騷動（如political agitation）。
turbulence	不可數名詞。混亂的政治或情緒狀態，和turmoil相似。最常指氣流的亂流。
commotion	突然發生吵鬧的行為。

Unit 66 散落，散布

StringNet語料庫出現次數

distribute	scatter	disperse	sprinkle	strew
3099	1529	824	544	316

distribute（vt.）

❖ 常用句型

> **S + distribute + O**

❖ 例句

Occupational welfare is not evenly distributed and does not cover the whole workforce.

職業福利並沒有平均分配，也沒有涵蓋所有勞動人口。

❖ 常用搭配詞

adv. + distributed

widely, evenly, equally, unevenly, normally, uniformly, randomly, well, airly, geographically, mainly, differentially, sparsely, freely, homogeneously, independently, increasingly identically, irregularly, originally, generally, equitably, patchily, parallel, carefully, rapidly, fully, badly, unfairly, thinly, liberally, readily, quickly, properly, erratically.

n. + be distributed

foundation, crop, money, products, tickets, company, publicity, system, power, dividends, water, copies, wealth, funds, population, cells, earnings, leaflets, reward, profits, seats, line, resources, photographs, protocols, press, target, weight, energy, books, questionnaire, booklet, news, remainder, software, pamphlet, production, curriculum, gas, work, letter, records, treaty.

scatter（vi./vt.）

❖ 常用句型

> **S + scatter（+ O）**

❖ 例句

Wheels and parts of the undercarriage of the cars were scattered along the track after the collision.

撞擊後這輛火車的車輪和底盤的零件沿著鐵軌散落滿地。

Churches may scatter the ashes in the graveyard or bury them according to the family's wishes.

教堂會依據家屬的願望把骨灰撒在墓園或埋在墓園。

The birds scattered as they heard the gunshot.

當鳥群聽到槍聲便四散飛去。

❖ 常用搭配詞

n. + be scattered

ashes, forces, houses, items, eggs, granules.

scatter the + _n._

   ashes, letters, rest, contest, seeds, stumps, papers, gravel, cheese.

adv. + scattered

   widely, thinly, forward, singly, liberally, doubly, inherently.

disperse（vi./vt.）

❖ 常用句型

> **S + disperse（+ O）**

❖ 例句

Police used tear gas to disperse the demonstrators.
警方用催淚瓦斯驅散示威群眾。

After midnight the crowd began to disperse.
過了午夜後群眾開始分散。

❖ 常用搭配詞

adv. + dispersed

   widely, geographically, quickly, finally, evenly, equally, spatially, violently, finely, rapidly, forcibly, easily, completely.

_n._ + be dispersed

   species, material, community, collections, oil, benefits.

disperse the + _n._

   crowds, slick, demonstrators, fog, oil, protesters.

sprinkle（vt.）

❖ 常用句型

> **S + sprinkle + O**

❖ 例句

She loves mango ice cream sprinkled with cashew nuts.
她喜歡芒果冰淇淋上面灑腰果顆粒。

❖ 常用搭配詞

sprinkled with + _n._
　　sugar, salt, cashew, stars.

sprinkle the + _n._
　　cheese, gelatin, top, flour, lawn, coffin.

strew（vt.）

❖ 常用句型

> **S + strew + O**

❖ 例句

The floor, desk, and chairs were strewn with books and papers.
地板，書桌，和椅子上到處散落著書本和紙張。

❖ 常用搭配詞

strewn + adv.

  about, all, everywhere, around.

n. + strewn with

  desk, floors, table, area, path, floor.

strew with + n.

  books, papers, swags, cigarette, rubbish, obstacles, rocks, corpses, wreckage, bodies.

綜合整理

distribute	及物動詞。有計畫性地把某物分散給人群或大範圍地分散。另外也指供貨給商家。
scatter	及物或不及物動詞。不規則地把某物散佈在某個範圍。另外也指人群或動物朝不同方向散開。
disperse	及物或不及物動詞。（使）人群或物品朝不同方向散開。
sprinkle	及物動詞。使水滴狀液體或許多小片或小塊物品潑灑落下。
strew	及物動詞。把物品分散於大範圍。

Unit 67 死亡

StringNet語料庫出現次數

die	perish
21328	393

die（vi.）

❖ 常用句型

> **S + die（prep. + N）**

❖ 例句

He died of lung cancer.
他死於肺癌。

❖ 常用搭配詞

n.（s）+ die

　people, father, mother, man, husband, children, person, men, woman, patient, son, Christ, king, habits, victim, animals, soldiers, pensioner, friends, body, population, trees.

die of + n.

　cancer, pneumonia, hunger, starvation, aids, asthma, radiation, shock, shock.

perish（vi.）

❖ 常用句型

S + perish（prep. + N）

❖ 例句

It is estimated that around 300 students perished in the shipping disaster.
估計約有三百位學生死於這場船難

❖ 常用搭配詞

perish in the + n.

　attempt, flames, waters, gutters, war, struggle.

n.（s） + perish

　goods, people, crew, hopes, species, men, goldfish, army.

綜合整理

die	死亡。主詞通常是人或動物。另外也表示聲音或笑容等消失停止。
perish	正式或文學用字。死亡、毀滅，或逐漸消失，尤其是死於意外或突然死亡（例如perish in the flames死於火災），主詞通常是人，有時也指動物或抽象名詞（如hope希望，democracy民主）。
另外decease n.也表示死亡，是法律用字（如at/after one's decease），因為語料庫收錄極少，所以在此不討論。	

Unit 68 醫治

StringNet語料庫出現次數

cure	heal
1095	797

cure（vi./vt.）

❖ 常用句型

> **S + cure + somebody（of something）**

❖ 例句

He was miraculously cured of the disease after one month.
一個月後他的病奇蹟似地被治好了。

❖ 常用搭配詞

cure the + n.
　　problem, patient, disease, ills, condition, anxiety, sickness, water, king.

adv. + cure
　　completely, fully, miraculously, easily, naturally, automatically.

heal（vi./vt.）

❖ 常用句型

> **S + heal（+ O）**

❖ 例句

A broken bone usually takes longer to heal than sprain.
通常骨折比扭傷需要花較長的時間痊癒。

❖ 常用搭配詞

n.（s）+ heal
　time, wounds, body, Jesus, ulcers, skin, scars, injuries, breach.

adv. + heal
　completely, eventually, gradually, finally, fully, really, quickly, freshly, instantly, properly.

heal the + n.
　wounds, breach, world, divisions, scars, past, split, pain.

綜合整理

cure	醫治疾病，使復原。另外也指改善困境。
heal	表示傷口等自行痊癒（不及物動詞），使某人恢復健康（及物動詞），尤其是藉著自然力量或祈禱，或是醫治心靈的傷痛（及物動詞或不及物動詞）。

Unit 69 醫師

StringNet語料庫出現次數

doctor	surgeon	physician
14540	1647	883

doctor（n.）

❖ 例句

You'd better go to the doctor about your migraine.
你最好去給醫生看你的偏頭痛。

❖ 常用搭配詞

n. + doctor

family, hospital, woman, witch, company, lady, army, street, police, school, prison, club, duty, reverend, village, emergency, student, camp, university, eye, hotel, home, training, radio, rescue.

adj. + doctor

junior, young, good, some, local, qualified, British, medical, private, senior, female, flying, homoeopathic, honorary, military, former, eminent, excellent, trained, experienced, leading, approved, famous, fellow, soviet, conventional, sympathetic, successful, orthodox, black, assistant, participating, caring, resident, independent, retired, competent, royal, overseas, fake, dedicated, native, personal, well-known, barefoot.

surgeon（n.）

❖ 例句

He took the injured dog to a veterinary surgeon.
他把那隻受傷的狗帶去給獸醫看。

❖ 常用搭配詞

n. + surgeon

police, house, brain, plastic, consultant, heart, veterinary, eye, transplant, general, trauma, tree, throat, army, mine, woman, county, command.

adj. + surgeon

veterinary, orthopedic, dental, eminent, ophthalmic, pioneering, british, assistant, pediatric, chief, senior, consultant, experienced, robotic, naval, brilliant, cosmetic, distinguished, resident, general, cardiac, qualified, neurological, inexperienced, military, consulting, honorary, junior.

physician（n.）

❖ 例句

You should talk to your personal physician before making the trip,
你去旅行之前應該先和你的私人醫生談一談。

❖ 常用搭配詞

adj. + physician

personal, general, experienced, German, royal, young, good, local, assistant, homoeopathic, eminent, senior, junior, resident, primary-care, skilled, leading, consultant, academic.

n. + physician

consultant, health, house, chest, study, family, community, care, street, hospital, master, university, household.

綜合整理

doctor	泛指一般讀過醫學院的醫生。
surgeon	外科醫生，動手術的醫生。
physician	美式英文的醫生，是doctor的正式用字。

Unit 70 醫療

StringNet語料庫出現次數

treatment	therapy
12973	2074

treatment（n.）

❖ 例句

The crippled Iranian went to the US seeking for medical treatment.

那位跛腳的伊朗人到美國尋求醫療。

❖ 常用搭配詞

adj. + treatment

medical, special, equal, preferential, effective, dental, surgical, active, psychiatric, conventional, appropriate, steroid, endoscopic, specific, harsh, fair, alternative, full, ill, initial, standard, rough, intensive, free, proper, current, general, detailed, follow-up, chemical, prolonged, conservative, private, regular, combined, separate, intermediate, subsequent, nutritional, long-term, compulsory, immediate, adequate, humane, dietary, generous, urgent, professional, systematic, extensive, residential, lenient, prompt, experimental, sensitive, remedial, curative, biological, radical, therapeutic, hygienic, aggressive, thorough, holistic, oral, comprehensive, veterinary.

<u>n.</u> + treatment

hospital, water, drug, laser, antibiotic, emergency, heat, maintenance, in-patient, acid, cancer, shock, physiotherapy, radiation, outpatient, priority, injection, hormone, replacement, insulin, radiotherapy, group, aids, chemotherapy, ulcer, aid, infertility, rescue, oxygen, alcohol, skin, health, routine, benchmark, scar, endoscopy, insemination, penicillin, nutrition, equilibrium, steam, reminder, protein, diabetes, diet, scalp, massage, stroke, dilatation, addiction.

therapy（n.）

❖ 例句

For many people group therapy can be more effective than individual therapy.

對許多人而言團體治療比個人治療還有效。

❖ 常用搭配詞

<u>adj.</u> + therapy

occupational, thrombolytic, cognitive, oral, complementary, triple, social, adjuvant, conventional, neural, adjunctive, natural, marital, intensive, individual, effective, personal, intravenous, sexual, dietary, prolonged, active, surgical, steroid, experimental, genetic, combined, holistic, supportive, diabetic, primal, nutritional, self-help, novel, aggressive, preventive.

<u>n.</u> + therapy

gene, speech, replacement, drug, family, group, regression, shock, rehydration, antibiotic, radiation, relaxation, art, oxygen, acid, behavior, cancer, maintenance, combination, laser, aversion, play, sex, hormone, ulcer, music, reminiscence, diet.

綜合整理

treatment	治療疾病或傷口。
therapy	療程，療法，時間比treatment長。

Unit 71 遺跡

StringNet語料庫出現次數

ruin	debris	remnant
1040	750	536

ruin（n.）

❖ 例句

There are numerous pictures of ruins of bombed houses in the photography exhibition.

在此攝影展中有許多被轟炸過的房屋廢墟的照片。

❖ 常用搭配詞

the ruin（s）of +（adj.）n.

castle, priory, empire, abbey, pyramid.

adj. + ruin

ancient, roman, smoking, monastic, smoldering, old, classical, utter, sad, complete, Greek, well-preserved, crumbling, magnificent, Mayan, medieval, roofless, 16-century, burning, charred, partial, beautiful, gothic, tumbled, inca, physical.

debris（n.）

❖ 例句

The debris of the lost plane was found after two years.
兩年後這架失蹤飛機的殘骸才被找到。

❖ 常用搭配詞

adj. + debris
  volcanic, flying, accumulated, nuclear, floating, human, harmless, soft, surrounding, burning.

n. + of debris
  pieces, amount, type, piles, bits, wall, mass, accumulation.

the debris of + n.
  erosion.

remnant（n.）

❖ 例句

The exhibition ends with the remnants of the statue of Stalin.
展覽的最後是一個殘破的史達林雕像。
He can make a new dish from remnants of a meal.
他可以用剩菜剩飯做出一道新料理。

❖ 常用搭配詞

adj. + remnants

  tatter, faint, shattered.

remnants of the + _n._

  past, storm.

綜合整理

ruin	可數名詞。建築物被毀壞後剩下的部分，如廢墟、遺跡。前面常接古文明的形容詞（如Roman ruins羅馬遺跡，Mayan ruins馬雅遺跡）。
debris	不可數名詞。某個物件被破壞之後剩下或四散的零碎部分，如碎石或殘骸。另外也指隨意棄置的垃圾。
remnant	可數名詞，通常是複數。遺跡、殘存、殘存者。某個物件被毀壞、使用、或吃掉之後剩下的小部分。

Unit 72 儀式

StringNet語料庫出現次數

ceremony	ritual	rite
2142	1422	648

ceremony（n.）

❖ 例句

Their wedding ceremony was held in a beautiful castle in French.

他們的婚禮在法國的一座美麗的城堡舉行。

❖ 常用搭配詞

n. + ceremony

opening, awards, wedding, marriage, initiation, presentation, tea, naming, signing, degree, funeral, installation, coronation, prize-giving, inauguration, swearing-in, dedication, fertility, burial, independence, launching, enthronement, commemoration, cremation, church, communion, exorcism, purification, court, medal, thanksgiving.

adj. + ceremony

religious, special, public, official, due, simple, formal, brief, civil, important, actual, short, annual, primitive, final, traditional, baptismal, elaborate, glittering, Christian, solemn, small, ritual, magic, pagan, national, televised, commemorative, stone-laying, symbolic, ancient, secret, sacred.

ritual（n.）

❖ 例句

The zoologist is interested in the study of bird mating rituals.
這位動物學家對於研究鳥類的求偶儀式有興趣。

❖ 常用搭配詞

n. + ritual

  initiation, fertility, headmaster, Sunday, courtship, spring, purification, court, family, temple, exorcism.

adj. + ritual

  religious, primitive, elaborate, ancient, social, annual, sacred, pagan, strange, mating, Christian, savage, solemn, tribal, Catholic, hideous, magic, sacrificial, ceremonial, bizarre, satanic, traditional.

rite（n.）

❖ 例句

The initiation rites for freshmen students in university often turn abusive.
在大學裡新生的社團入會儀式往往有虐待性。

❖ 常用搭配詞

adj. + rite

last, religious, primitive, eastern, ancient, funerary, sacred, holy, magical, traditional, forgotten, catholic, baptismal, sacrificial, proper, idolatrous, healing.

n. + rite

fertility, initiation, funeral, puberty, burial, communion.

綜合整理

ceremony	重要社交或宗教場合的正式儀式。大型儀式常用此字（如inauguration ceremony就職典禮，coronation ceremony加冕典禮）。
ritual	重要社交或宗教場合的儀式、儀式程序，和rite相似。另外也衍伸為日常生活的例行公事。原始或邪教的儀式常用此字（如tribal ritual部落儀式，satanic ritual和撒旦有關的儀式）。
rite	儀式，尤其是宗教儀式。

Unit 73 疑心的

StringNet語料庫出現次數

suspicious	doubtful	skeptical	dubious	suspect
1300	1212	754	699	122

suspicious（adj.）

❖ 例句

They are suspicious of foreigners.

他們對外國人很多疑。

They caught a suspicious man in the woods.

他們在樹林中捉到一名可疑的男子。

❖ 常用搭配詞

a suspicious + n.

　　look, glance, mind, death, package, person, glare, character, manner, nature, woman, car, light.

suspicious of（det.）+ n.

　　circumstances, people, attempts, motives, injection, king, taste.

v. + suspicious

　　become, look, remain, feel, seem.

adv. + suspicious

deeply, highly, naturally, extremely, immediately, instantly, increasingly, rightly, suddenly, profoundly, especially, remotely, initially, intensely, thoroughly.

doubtful（adj.）

❖ 例句

It's doubtful whether anyone can survive the snow storm in the mountain.
令人懷疑是否有人能度過這場山上的暴風雪。
She is still doubtful if she should quit her job.
她仍然懷疑是否該辭掉工作。

❖ 常用搭配詞

doubtful + n.

debts, cases, validity, value, authenticity, expression, origin, quality, claim, relevance, premise, loans, efficacy, look, legality, ground, title, smile, advances, birth, practices, honor, voice, morals, service, stamina, statement, privilege, part, taste, species, points.

v. + doubtful

look, seem, sound, remain, feel.

adv. + doubtful

extremely, highly, equally, increasingly.

skeptical（adj.）

❖ 例句

A lot of people are very skeptical about Darwin's theory of evolution.
很多人很懷疑達爾文的進化論。
His new discovery in Africa received a skeptical response from the
archaeologists and historians.
考古學家和歷史學家對他在非洲的新發現的反應是懷疑的。

❖ 常用搭配詞

skeptical + n.
　　argument, attitude, view, eyebrow, observers, look, questions, audience,
　　philosopher, reader, public, stance, eye, doubts, response, age.

v. + skeptical
　　remain, look, feel, become, sound.

adv. + skeptical
　　highly, deeply, extremely, increasingly, openly, initially, slightly, fairly,
　　rightly, particularly, radically, downright, mildly, normally.

dubious（adj.）

❖ 例句

He said, looking dubious, "Are you sure?"
他以懷疑的表情說：「你確定嗎?」
Some citizens are dubious about whether the mayor will keep his promise.
有些市民懷疑市長是否會信守他的承諾。

❖ 常用搭配詞

dubious + n.

value, penalty, reputation, proposition, nature, legality, means, taste, business, benefit, provenance, privilege, validity, claim, accounting, advantage, status, elements, sources, methods, practices, asset, confessions, substances, circumstances, position, title, character, relevance, activities, dealing, refereeing, side, authenticity, material, compliment, goods, credit, reasons, statistics, way, delights, tactics, record, history, argument, role, company, grounds, intent, achievement, enterprise.

v. + dubious

look, render, sound.

adv. + dubious

highly, extremely, distinctly, morally, slightly, equally, initially.

suspect（adj.）

❖ 例句

The selling tactics used by the company were deemed to be highly suspect.

這公司的銷售策略被認為是相當有問題的。

The virgin birth is highly suspect for non-Christians.

對於非基督而言處女懷孕是很可疑的。

❖ 常用搭配詞

suspect + n.

　motives.

n.（s）+ be suspect

　figures, organizations.

adv. + suspect

　highly, particularly, slightly, automatically, equally, increasingly, clearly, deeply.

綜合整理

suspicious	可以形容人和事物。形容人的時候是表示懷疑的、多疑的，不信任某個人事物，懷疑某人不誠實或有犯案，主詞是人。形容事物的時候表示可疑的，令人懷疑可能是違法或危險的（如look suspicious 看起來很可疑），後面常接表示事物的名詞（如suspicious package 可疑的包裹）。
doubtful	可以形容人和事物。形容人的時候是表示不確定某件事情的真實性或不確定是否該做某件事情。形容事物的時候表示令人懷疑是否是真的、是否會發生、是否會成功、或是否是好的（如doubtful authenticity令人懷疑的真實性）。
skeptical	懷疑的、不相信的、多疑的（如skeptical attitude懷疑的態度）。
dubious	可以形容人和事物。形容人的時候和doubtful一樣表示不確定某件事情的真實性或不確定是否該做某件事情（look dubious 看起來有疑心、不確定）。形容事物的時候表示令人懷疑是否是誠實的、正確的、或真實的。
suspect	可疑的，可能不是誠實的，或可能有問題的（如suspect figures 可疑的數字）。後面可接名詞表示可能是有炸彈或危險的（如suspect motives 可疑的動機）。當名詞時表示嫌疑犯。

Unit 74 野蠻的

StringNet語料庫出現次數

wild	savage	barbaric
5322	613	165

wild（adj.）

❖ 例句

These college students wasted their time in wild parties.

這些大學生把他們的時間浪費在狂野的派對裡。

❖ 常用搭配詞

wild + n.

night, game, parties, beast, world, state, boy, idea, eyes, nature, moment, ride, ancestors, applause, excitement, beauty, pleasure, urge, people, weather, women, days, look, rumor, show, enthusiasm, exaggeration, joy, desire, passion, specimens, time, instincts, behavior, style, cheers, dancing, warriors, cry, ways, reaction, tribes, surge, pride, magic, emotions, punch.

savage（adj.）

❖ 例句

He was seriously injured in the savage attack.
他在這場野蠻的攻擊中受到重傷。
The scholar studied the ancient savage rituals in some African tribes.
這位學者研究古代非洲部落的野蠻儀式。

❖ 常用搭配詞

savage + n.

attack, blow, beasts, world, anger, look, reprisals, creature, struggle, dogs, mind, death, war, winter, man, pleasure, gesture, side, amusement, ritual, place, eyes, joy, nights, murders, test, penalties, club, rites, customs, strength, society, scene, assault, ways, rioting, fighting, practices, passion, beating, hatred, feud.

barbaric（adj.）

❖ 例句

The President condemned the barbaric acts of the terrorists.
總統譴責這些恐怖份子的野蠻行為。

❖ 常用搭配詞

barbaric + n.

practice, acts, sport, crimes, carnage, activity, oppression, tribes.

綜合整理

wild	行為暴力不受控制的，狂野的。另外表示其他多種意義如野生的，未開發的，所以在語料庫出現次數頻繁。
savage	暴力殘酷的，野蠻未開化的。
barbaric	暴力殘酷的。

Unit 75 煙霧

StringNet語料庫出現次數

smoke	mist	fog	haze	smog
2707	1187	879	355	169

smoke（n.）

❖ 例句

He put a cigarette in his mouth and exhaled a wreath of smoke in the air.
他把香菸放進嘴哩，然後呼出一圈煙霧。
Billowing smoke came from the house on fire.
從失火的房子冒出陣陣濃煙。

❖ 常用搭配詞

adj. + smoke

black, blue, white, acrid, thick, belching, dark, dense, billowing, choking, grey, sleep-safe, carbolic, holy, stale, toxic, holy, pungent, inhaled, aromatic, heavy, poisonous, choking, colored, exhaled, pouring, faint, emitting, swirling.

n. + smoke

cigarette, tobacco, cigar, wood, exhaust, sidestream, coal, diesel, factory, fire, pipe, oil, cannabis, bonfire.

n. + smoke

cloud, puff, pall, wisp, column, plume, stream, haze, pillar, spiral, veils.

mist（n.）

❖ 例句

She likes to take a walk in the wood in the morning when the sun shines through the mist.

她喜歡在早晨陽光穿過霧氣時在樹林散步。

❖ 常用搭配詞

adj. +mist

thick, heavy, grey, fine, white, red, Scotch, swirling, early, thin, slight, faint, blue, dark, tenuous, black, damp, clinging, floating, watery, early-morning, light, cold, sunlit, wet, pale, spectral, dense, golden, sudden, rolling.

n. + mist

morning, sea, evening, dawn, gel, acid, ground, glen, silver, autumn.

mist + n.

patches.

mists of + n.

time, sleep, history, tradition.

fog（n.）

❖ 例句

Her flight was delayed because of thick fog.
她的班機因為濃霧而延遲。

❖ 常用搭配詞

adj. + fog

　　thick, freezing, dense, patchy, swirling, heavy, white, blue, early, perpetual, icy, shifting, coastal, damp, warm, grey.

n. + fog

　　winter, sea, hill, London, night.

fog + n.

　　patches, lamps, lights, horn, warning, line.

haze（n.）

❖ 例句

The horsemen disappeared in a haze of dust.
那群騎馬的男士消失在一陣灰塵的煙霧中。
Everything looked blurry in the heat haze above the African fields.
在非洲草原上的熱氣使每個東西看起來都是模糊的。

❖ 常用搭配詞

a haze of + n.

dust, heat.

n. + haze

heat, smoke, sun, dust.

smog（n.）

❖ 例句

The smog emergency forced China Government to shut Daquing City, one of Northeastern China's largest cities.

霾害迫使中國政府關閉大慶市，也是中國東北方最大的城市之一。

Photochemical smog is the chemical reaction of sunlight, nitrogen oxides and volatile organic compounds in the atmosphere, which leaves noxious mixture of air pollutants.

光化學煙霧是陽光、二氧化氮、和揮發性有機物質在大氣層中產生的化學反應，會造成有毒的空氣汙染源。

❖ 常用搭配詞

adj. + smog

photochemical, urban.

n. + smog

London, winter, ozone.

smog + n.

alert, levels, problem, monster, tax, emergencies.

綜合整理

smoke	不可數名詞。因為燃燒而產生的白色、灰色、或黑色的煙。
mist	可數或不可數名詞。水氣造成的、無法透視的雲霧或霧氣，和fog相似，尤其指清晨的霧氣。常用複數表示抽象意義（如lost in the mists of time 年代久遠不可考）。
fog	可數或不可數名詞。水氣造成的、無法透視的雲霧或霧氣，和mist相似，後面常接名詞表示和濃霧相關的事物（如fog warning濃霧警報，fog lamp霧燈）。
haze	單數不可數名詞，無法透視的煙霧、塵霧。
smog	可數或不可數名詞。工廠或汽車排出骯髒的煙霧。

Unit 76 嚴格的

StringNet語料庫出現次數

strict	rigid	stringent	stern
2384	1409	489	411

strict（adj.）

❖ 例句

The teacher is very strict about students coming to class on time.
那位老師很嚴格要求學生準時到課。
This country has very strict laws against theft and vandalism.
這國家關於偷竊和故意破壞公物的法律很嚴格。

❖ 常用搭配詞

strict + n.

rules, liability, sense, control, limits, instruction, adherence, discipline, conditions, diet, guidelines, criteria, regime, standards, orders, regulations, separation, interpretation, supervision, requirements, timetable, training, division, confidentiality, observance, attention, application, laws, compliance, enforcement, censorship, security, accordance, approach, terms, hierarchy, policy, definition, curfew, planning, procedures, routine, government, form, deadline, justice, provisions, upbringing, confines, insistence, specifications, man, segregation, implementation, regimen, quarantine, logic, schedules, Baptist, line, fairness, father, wording, version, licensing, conformity, timetables, curfew, tempo, privacy.

adv. + strict

fairly, less, particularly, increasingly, really, equally, comparatively, relatively, unnecessarily.

rigid（adj.）

❖ 例句

She is tired of her father's rigid adherence to Jewish law.
她對於父親嚴格堅守猶太教的律法感到厭煩。

❖ 常用搭配詞

rigid + n.

rules, structure, adherence, control, system, distinction, separation, packaging, division, line, discipline, stance, hierarchy, pattern, application, framework, conventions, definition, approach, way, policy, dichotomy, dogma, standard, belief, orthodoxy, drill, timetable, requirements, routines, principles, training, enforcement, planning, hostility, boundaries, diet.

adv. + rigid

fairly, relatively, absolutely, extremely, totally, entirely, suddenly, excessively.

stringent（adj.）

❖ 例句

There are stringent controls on pollution from all factories.
針對所有工廠的汙染有嚴格的控管。

❖ 常用搭配詞

stringent + n.

conditions, criteria, regulations, controls, tests, rules, measures, standards, requirements, quality, security, terms, criticism, planning, cuts, targets, contract, restrictions, government, discipline, policy, provisions, demands, austerity, constraints, penalties, precautions, obligation, limits, budget.

adv. + stringent

increasingly, fairly, equally, highly, supposedly.

stern（adj.）

❖ 例句

The company gave its competitor a stern warning.
這家公司給它的競爭對手嚴正的警告。
His math teacher is a tern man who rarely smiles.
他的數學老師是一位不苟言笑、嚴厲的男士。

❖ 常用搭配詞

stern + _n._

warning, test, voice, line, look, face, lecture, eye, duty, measures, expression, gaze, authority, mother, words, features, resistance, attitude.

adv. + stern

rather, more.

綜合整理

strict	形容一個人期望他人服從命令或他所說的話，也形容規則或命令很嚴格，一定要遵守。後面名詞可以是人或非人。
rigid	形容方法或制度嚴格不能被改變，或是人不願意改變自己的想法或行為。後面名詞通常不是人。
stringent	形容法律或標準嚴格，一定要遵守。後面名詞通常不是人。
stern	嚴厲，尤其是在表示反對（如stern warning嚴正的警告）。後面名詞可以是人或非人。

Unit 77 引誘，吸引

StringNet語料庫出現次數

attract	lure	seduce	entice
6308	481	419	274

attract（vt.）

❖ 常用句型

> S + attract + O

❖ 例句

Sometimes people may do crazy things to attract attention.
有的時候人們會因為想引起別人注意而做出瘋狂的事情。
Many young people were attracted to bungee jumps in Australia.
許多人被澳洲的高空彈跳所吸引。

❖ 常用搭配詞

attract +（det.）n.

attention, people, visitors, support, interest, criticism, customers, women, tourists, students, females, investment, business, men, crowds, investors, members, funds, publicity, children, funding, comment, money, audiences, tax, birds, viewers, fish, players, media, dust, buyers, deposits, advertising, readers, workers, votes, residents, supporters, clients, offers, immigrants, insects, sponsorship, parents, bids, companies, passengers, migrants, praise, suspicion, males, sympathy, mates, crime, candidates, hostility, flies, press, artist, admiration, trouble, controversy, shareholders, animals, trade, predators, participants, delegates, glances, shoppers, youth, pilgrims, thieves, experts, inventors, savings, passers-by, donations.

attract + one's n.
attention, mates, eye, share, support, prey.

lure（vt.）

❖ 常用句型

> **S+ lure + O**

❖ 例句

The religious leader warned young people not to be lured into cults.
那位宗教領袖警告年輕人不要被引誘加入邪教。

❖ 常用搭配詞

lure the + n.
birds, reader, boy.

lured by the + n.
promise, rumors, song, smile.

seduce（vt.）

❖ 常用句型

> **S + seduce + O**

❖ 例句

He has learnt his lesson through being seduced by beautiful women.
他已經從被美貌的女性誘惑當中學到教訓。

I am seduced by the city's romance and vitality.
我被這城市的浪漫與活力迷住。

❖ 常用搭配詞

be seduced by the + <u>n.</u>
  prospect, city, promise.

seduce +（det.）<u>n.</u>
  enemy, daughter, wife, viewer, man, Christian, girl, husband.

entice （vt.）

❖ 常用句型

> **S+ entice + O**

❖ 例句

He came up with a brilliant idea to entice customers to his shop.
他想到一個妙計來吸引顧客上門。

❖ 常用搭配詞

entice +（det.） n.

　customers, people, others, dog, sponsorship, females, public, reader,

綜合整理

attract	吸引，使人對某個東西有興趣或想要參與某件事情。也表示吸引異性。在語料庫中時常表示招來、招致，後面的受詞有正面的意義（如attract attention吸引人的注意，attract investment吸引投資），也有負面的意義（attract criticism招來批評，attract suspicion引起懷疑）。
lure	引誘人去做某件事情，尤其是用巧計使人去做錯誤或危險的事情。也表示挖角或搶別家商店的顧客。
seduce	誘使別人和自己發生性關係，尤其是以間接的方式，常用被動語態。也表示使某事物看起來有趣或吸引人的。
entice	以利誘的方式使人去做某事，尤其指吸引顧客。

Unit 78 隱藏，隱瞞

StringNet語料庫出現次數

hide	conceal
5961	1632

hide（vi./vt.）

❖ 常用句型

> **S + hide（+ O）（+ from somebody）**

❖ 例句

The man's face was mostly hidden by an upturned collar and a hat pulled well down.

那男士的臉大部分被豎起來的領子和垂下的帽子遮住。

You could not hide from God.

你無法躲避上帝。

❖ 常用搭配詞

hide the + _n._

fact, truth, gun, sun, book, pain, brandy, money, material, house, flush, evidence, light, complexity, fear, blemish, shock, view, key, face, blush, presence, killer, identity, hurt, look, smell, ball, failure, bottle, plumbing.

hide one's + _n._

feelings, astonishment, disappointment, frustration, surprise.

adv. + hide

well, half, almost, completely, largely, carefully, partly, partially, probably, safely, hardly, barely, scarcely, normally, previously, quickly, entirely, totally, temporarily, cleverly, merely, simply, naturally, mostly, easily, fully, successfully, consciously, purposely, modestly, effectively, hastily, deeply.

conceal（vt.）

❖ 常用句型

> **S + conceal + O**

❖ 例句

She attempted to conceal the fact that she was pregnant.
她企圖隱瞞她懷孕的事實。
She could not conceal her feelings any longer.
她再也無法隱藏她的感情。

❖ 常用搭配詞

conceal the + _n._

fact, truth, extent, identity, body, evidence, knowledge, work, pain, money, birth, bottom, degree, reality.

conceal one's + n.

    surprise, disappointment, love, distress, hair, astonishment, enthusiasm.

adv. + conceal

    barely, completely, deliberately, party, successfully, dishonestly, scarcely, easily, cleverly, effectively, carefully, fully, simply, frequently, shrewdly, possibly, politely, cunningly, safely, previously, merely, doubtless, partially, apparently, normally.

綜合整理

hide	及物或不及物動詞。當及物動詞時表示把某人或某物隱藏在某處或遮住使不能被看見，常用被動語態。也表示隱瞞心中的感受。當不及物動詞時表示躲起來。
conceal	及物動詞。小心翼翼地隱藏起來，也表示隱藏感情或隱瞞真相，常用在否定句。

Unit 79 陰暗的

StringNet語料庫出現次數

dark	gloomy	dim	murky
10618	688	671	235

dark（adj.）

❖ 例句

He saw someone sitting in the dark corner of the room.
他看到有一個人坐在屋子裡陰暗的角落。
The title of his new book is "the dark side of human nature."
他新書的標題是「人性的黑暗面」。

❖ 常用搭配詞

dark + n.

hair, eyes, head, green, glasses, side, ages, room, night, face, man, suit, matter, wood, shape, brows, corner, shadow, water, lashes, skin, secret, shapes, chocolate, horse, street, forest, power, tunnel, stain, winter, cave, forces, road, realm, world, blood, sea, smoke, space, lady, deeds, corridor, continent, wings, figures, smudges, cloak, complexion, pit, glance, streaks, period, navy, outline, alley, stone, hallway, bar, country, beer, leaves, time, liquid, magic, bay, years, gold, body, shades, lake, emptiness, earth, people, picture, journey, marks, car, city, angel, leather, mood, sorcery, urine, mist, brick, cellar, coffee, snow, metal, nature, bruise, spectacles, flood, humor, bomber, sunburst, laughter, heart, undercurrent, oil, gleam, smile, castle, paint, paths, comedy.

adv. + dark

slightly, significantly, gradually, generally, usually.

gloomy（adj.）

❖ 例句

In the lecture the speaker painted a gloomy picture of the future economy of our country.

在演講中這位講員指出我們國家經濟的未來前景一片黯淡。

There is a gloomy atmosphere in the painting.

這幅畫中有一股陰沉的氣氛。

❖ 常用搭配詞

gloomy + n.

picture, news, view, thoughts, predictions, room, prognosis, forecast, silence, interior, conclusion, place, prospects, future, day, atmosphere, passage, world, house, mood, reading, corridors, weather, winter, talk, affair, sky, chill, garden, background, report, corners, morning, side, street, cathedral, outlook,

adv. + gloomy

rather, particularly, equally, increasingly, fairly, uniformly, distinctly, terribly.

dim（adj.）

❖ 例句

Only the dim light from the distant lighthouse could be seen in the sea.
在海上唯一看得到的只有遙遠燈塔上微弱的光。
He saw a dim figure coming toward him.
他看到一個模糊的身影朝他走來。

❖ 常用搭配詞

dim + n.

light, view, statement, sum, lighting, glow, stars, interior, memory, room, shape, recollection, outlines, blur, recesses, figure, past, sense, corner, sky, hall, world, chamber, vision, streets, constellation, lantern, mountains, way, idea, stairs, feeling.

adv. + dim

extremely, slightly, particularly, fairly, sufficiently.

murky（adj.）

❖ 例句

There is no fish in the murky river.
這條漆黑汙濁的河裡沒有魚。

❖ 常用搭配詞

murky + n.

waters, water, past, world, depths, green, river, night, affair, people, rainwater, winter, area, conditions, sea, day, darkness, clouds, environment, light, blackness, pools.

adv. + murky

extremely.

綜合整理

dark	光線或顏色很暗，黑暗神祕或邪惡的。
gloomy	令人覺得陰沉悲哀（如gloomy atmosphere陰沉的氣氛），前途暗淡無希望的（gloomy future黯淡的未來）。
dim	光線暗淡，因為太遠或太暗而模糊不清（如dim figure模糊的身影）。
murky	黑暗混濁，常用來形容河水。複雜難懂，或背地裡暗藏不法或謊言的。

Unit 80 影響

StringNet語料庫出現次數

effect	influence	impact
33263	9269	7616

effect（n.）

❖ 例句

Is it possible to close the ozone gap and save the world from the greenhouse effect?

有可能修補臭氧層並拯救全世界免於溫室效應嗎?

The government then were not conscious of the devastating effect of low birth rate on schools.

當時的政府沒有意識到少子化對學校的毀滅性影響。

❖ 常用搭配詞

adj. + effect

little, adverse, immediate, overall, direct, profound, cumulative, desired, opposite, devastating, knock-on, beneficial, positive, detrimental, main, practical, full, combined, maximum, negative, damaging, protective, major, serious, marked, powerful, inhibitory, deleterious, likely, lasting, disastrous, long-term, total, intended, small, obvious, stimulatory, therapeutic, substantial, psychological, causal, visual, equivalent, strong, cooling, original, limited, calming, large, harmful, reverse, specific, traumatic, natural, emotional, independent, depressing, magical, potential, economic, apparent, finished, synergistic, decisive, gravitational, distorting, permanent, financial, soothing, destabilizing, decorative, word-superiority, pathogenic, political, physical, drastic, healing, destructive, hypnotic, negligible, catastrophic, short-term, corrosive, initial, clear, odd, visible, debilitating, inevitable, measurable, double, expressive, local, stunning, phenotypic, selective, social, additive, sobering, crippling, ultimate, liberating, discernible, marginal, pertinent, dominant, disturbing, minimal, relaxing, disruptive, inflationary, broad, crucial, overshadowing, expansionary, pervasive, neutral, increasing, mood-altering, seasonal, restrictive, detectable, chemical, mental, enormous, contrary, average, braking, far-reaching, subtle, aesthetic, ironic, temporary, delicate, warming, ideological, causative.

<u>n.</u> + effect

greenhouse, side, deterrent, substitution, domino, multiplier, inhibition, disincentive, ripple, field, demonstration, ground, backwash, balance, drying, halo, heating, cohort, snowball, treatment, laterality, output, incentive, observer, learning, cushioning, shock, bandwagon, cascade, demand, surface, moon, expectancy, context, temperature, dilution, heather, antibiotic, reminiscence.

<u>v.</u> + an effect

have, produce, create, show, call, cause, achieve, exert, make, find.

influence（n.）

❖ 例句

Smart phones exert a powerful influence over our lives.
智慧型手機對我們的生活產生強大的影響。

❖ 常用搭配詞

adj. + influence

undue, political, major, considerable, powerful, significant, strong, direct, profound, growing, outside, external, cultural, bad, French, social, communist, main, decisive, dominant, formative, personal, environmental, local, positive, negative, foreign, big, pervasive, early, increasing, religious, enormous, human, potential, Soviet, musical, economic, independent, lasting, evil, good, restraining, causal, disruptive, crucial, calming, potent, relative, parental, moderating, pernicious, huge, destructive, genetic, sufficient, predominant, substantial, various, tremendous, ideological, international, obvious, determining, overwhelming, stabilizing, royal, intellectual, historical, declining, long-term, immense, combined, mutual, diverse, global, guiding, Christian, marked, total, theoretical, controlling, widespread, maternal, structural, climatic, corrupting, urban, adverse, behavioral, moral, democratic, harmful, overriding, enduring, demoralizing, broad, limited, commercial, massive, benign, liberating, soothing, warming, immediate, disturbing, contemporary, subtle, overall, contextual, national, unconscious, top-down, conflicting, excessive, constructive, sinister, practical, gravitational, semantic, regional, benevolent, public.

n. + influence

family, government, union, US, media, world, music, group, authority, market, church, treasury, policy, structure, sex, culture, design.

v. + an influence on

have, exert.

impact（n.）

❖ 例句

They are waiting for the result of environmental impact assessment.
他們在等待環境影響評估的結果。

❖ 常用搭配詞

adj. + impact

environmental, significant, major, full, immediate, direct, economic, likely, considerable, visual, adverse, potential, negative, profound, overall, dramatic, social, political, initial, maximum, enormous, limited, emotional, main, devastating, human, strong, positive, substantial, tremendous, serious, high, powerful, lasting, marginal, little, severe, regional, huge, long-term, practical, psychological, minimal, physical, cumulative, combined, ecological, massive, future, actual, financial, large, obvious, inflationary, personal, relative, detrimental, disproportionate, cultural, beneficial, low, international, public, total, growing, negligible, fundamental, far-reaching, electoral, instant, disastrous, geographical, aggregate, continuing, perceived, overwhelming, sufficient, shattering, sudden, short-term, reduced, decisive, critical, biological, sharp, heavy, frontal, sheer, revolutionary, damaging, local, genetic, stunning, eventual, global, consequent, momentous, causal, theoretical, minor, apparent.

 n. + impact

employment, health, policy, traffic, market, environment, shock, pollution.

 v. + an impact

make, have, create, achieve, produce.

綜合整理

effect	可數或不可數名詞。一個事件或行動所造成的改變、效果，常用在身心醫療上（如sobering effect提神效果，side effect副作用）。
influence	可數或不可數名詞。對人的思想行為、或對一件事情發展的影響力，特別指自然產生非刻意造成的影響，常用在道德信仰上（如religious influence信仰的影響，moral influence道德上的影響）。也表示有影響力的人事物。
impact	可數名詞。某個事件或情況對人事物的影響、衝擊。常用在生態環境（如environmental impact對生態環境的影響，geographic impact地理上的影響）或突然的衝擊（sudden impact突發的影響）。另外也表示撞擊。

Unit 81 污染

StringNet語料庫出現次數

pollution	contamination
4140	637

pollution（n.）

❖ 例句

Air pollution in our country has been increasing for a decade.
在過去十年我們國家的空氣汙染一直增加。
The factory was fined for failing to control water pollution.
這工廠因為沒做好水汙染控管而遭罰鍰。

❖ 常用搭配詞

adj. + pollution

environmental, atmospheric, industrial, marine, integrated, chemical, severe, major, accidental, spiritual, resulting, agricultural, global, coastal, airborne, local, tradeable, visual, photochemical, radioactive, existing, heavy, ritual, expensive, reported, organic, moral, genetic, persistent, lethal, regional, man-made, biological, deliberate.

n. + pollution

air, water, oil, noise, nitrate, river, lead, ozone, odor, sewage, sulphur, sea, smoke, traffic, vehicle, acid, rain, groundwater, car, dioxide, exhaust, particle, atmosphere, gulf, source, fuel, transport, city, farm, soil.

v. +（det.）pollution

  reduce, monitor, tackle, control, curb, combat, limit, prevent, calculate, cause.

contamination（n.）

❖ 例句

The residents of this island are worried about the danger of contamination from radioactive wastes.

這個島上的居民很擔心放射物質廢料造成汙染的危險。

Increasing the dose of insecticide runs the risk of increasing environmental contamination.

增加殺蟲劑的劑量會增加汙染環境的風險。

❖ 常用搭配詞

adj. + contamination

  radioactive, environmental, possible, internal, salivary, bacterial, natural, moral, airborne, massive, serious, industrial, unavoidable, outside, toxic, extensive, earthly, organic, widespread.

n. + contamination

  pasture, water, food, surface, metal, dioxin, lead, soil, cross, chloride, blood, land, skin, radiation, mercury, waster, product, pesticide, carbon, grass, sediment.

v. + the contamination

  prevent, avoid, tolerate, increase, spread, cause.

綜合整理

pollution	使空氣、水、土壤等變髒或具有危險性，因而不適合人類使用。也表示汙染物。
contamination	藉由化學物質或毒物使某個地方或物品變髒或具有傷害性。

Unit 82 挖掘

StringNet語料庫出現次數

dig	excavate	unearth
2651	376	263

dig（vi./vt.）

❖ 常用句型

S + dig（+ O）

❖ 例句

They dug a hole in the garden to bury the dead bird.

他們在花園中挖了一個洞來埋葬那隻死去的鳥。

❖ 常用搭配詞

dig + n.

　trenches, holes, graves, tunnels, wells, ditches, canals, mines, pits, burrows, stone.

dig + adv.

　deeply, rapidly, painfully, savagely, firmly, frantically.

excavate（vt.）

❖ 常用句型

> **S + excavate + O**

❖ 例句

The Mao Gong Ding was excavated in Anhui Province, Mainland China, in 1957.

毛公鼎於1957年在中國大陸安徽省被挖掘出來。

❖ 常用搭配詞

excavate the + n.

　site, remains.

n. + be excavated

　site, example, building, tunnel.

unearth（vt.）

❖ 常用句型

> **S + unearth + O**

❖ 例句

Human skeletons and a cannon-ball have been unearthed in the garden.
在那個花園裡挖掘出幾具人類骨骸和一個舊式砲彈。

❖ 常用搭配詞

unearth the + _n._
　　remains, cause, laws.

_n._ + be unearthed
　　evidence, stone, skeleton.

綜合整理

dig	用鏟子或手在地面挖洞、或把土或雪挖走。片語dig in one's heels表示不肯妥協。
excavate	表示考古學家或科學家小心翼翼把古代器物從地下挖掘出來。
unearth	從地下挖掘出來。另外也表示揭露、發現，出現語料庫中的句子大多是此意。

Unit 83 危險的

StringNet語料庫出現次數

dangerous	hazardous	risky	precarious	perilous
5626	714	705	342	163

dangerous（adj.）

❖ 例句

The sharp bend in the road is notoriously dangerous.

那條路上的那著急轉彎是出了名的危險。

❖ 常用搭配詞

adv. + dangerous

potentially, extremely, highly, particularly, really, positively, downright, possibly, incredibly, politically, increasingly, terribly, inherently, obviously, immediately, notoriously, slightly, fairly, sufficiently, genuinely, exceedingly, seriously, desperately, physically, sexually, exceptionally, allegedly, undoubtedly, appallingly.

dangerous + n.

thing, situation, place, substances, dogs, man, driving, precedent, drugs, levels, chemicals, conditions, classes, work, practice, road, enemy, job, time, position, liaisons, products, animals, business, area, species, state, waste, moment, operation, world, junctions, part, consequences, corner, stuff, territory, illusion, waters, illness, sport, weapons, task, pesticides, environment, power, criminals, people, opponent, woman, journey, activities, behaviors, faults, cross, step, nonsense, life, occupation, objects, type, circumstances, games, years, course, policy, fumes, idea, reputation, maneuver, predator, tendency, traffic, industry, act, glint, word, exhibitions, undertaking, method, items, toxins, move, effects, side-effects, player, pastime, seas, nature.

hazardous（adj.）

❖ 例句

Environmentalists condemned plans for a hazardous waste storage site on the river bank.
環保人士譴責在河岸邊設立危險廢棄物存放位址的計畫。

❖ 常用搭配詞

hazardous + n.

waste, materials, chemicals, substances, journey, undertaking, occupation, business, properties, sites, goods, situations, operation, nature, task, industries, cargo, pesticides, products, road, installations, activities, place, environments, sports, part, plants, work, air, venture, process, ingredients, trip, voyages, liquid, enterprise.

adv. + hazardous

potentially, extremely, particularly, environmentally, possibly.

risky（adj.）

❖ 例句

All investment activities are inherently risky.
所有的投資活動本質上都是有風險的。

❖ 常用搭配詞

risky + n.

business, situation, junctions, exemplars, activities, investments, ventures, thing, projects, behavior, strategy, undertaking, sport, prospect, events, assets, woods, decision, policy, aspects, bid, game, securities, proposition, goods, markets, clients, situation, exercise, enterprise.

adv. + risky

highly, extremely, inherently, particularly, increasingly, decidedly, generally, potentially, obviously, politically.

precarious（adj.）

❖ 例句

The senator's political position was extremely precarious.
那位參議員的政治地位岌岌可危。

❖ 常用搭配詞

precarious + n.

   position, existence, living, balance, basis, hold, state, way, future, situation, victory, employment, viability, independence, nature, agreement, life, economy.

adv. + precarious

   financially, increasingly.

perilous（adj.）

❖ 例句

The children were fascinated by the stories of the perilous adventure of ancient heroes.

這些小孩深深著迷於古代英雄危機四伏的冒險故事。

❖ 常用搭配詞

perilous + n.

   journey, position, state, situation, way, sea, circumstances, angle, descent, passage, time, business, track, place, night, adventure.

adv. + perilous

   more, less, too.

綜合整理

dangerous	可能傷害或殺害生命的。
hazardous	危險的，尤其是危及健康或安全的（如hazardous air對健康有害的空氣，hazardous liquid危險的液體，例如易燃液體）。
risky	隨時有危險可能發生，和dangerous相似。
precarious	處在危險不穩定、可能很容易或是很快會變成更糟糕的狀況（如precarious peace岌岌可危的和平）。
perilous	非常危險。文學或正式用字。

Unit 84 危及

StringNet語料庫出現次數

endanger	jeopardize
453	262

endanger（vt.）

❖ 常用句型

> **S + endanger + O**

❖ 例句

Smoking during pregnancy can endanger the baby's health.
在懷孕期間吸菸可能會危及嬰孩的健康。

❖ 常用搭配詞

endanger the + _n._

　lives, safety, health, survival, future, fabric, position, security.

adv. + endanger

　highly, thereby, greatly, seriously, actually, possibly.

jeopardize（vt.）

❖ 常用句型

> **S + jeopardize + O**

❖ 例句

The current brain drain crisis can jeopardize the future of the country.
目前的人才外流危機可能會危及這個國家的未來。

❖ 常用搭配詞

jeopardize the + _n._
    future, chances, country, existence, plant, success.

adv. + jeopardize
    seriously.

綜合整理

endanger	使某個人事物處於可能被傷害、損壞、或毀滅的危險。
Jeopardize	造成失去或破壞某個重要事物的風險。

Unit 85 圍繞

StringNet語料庫出現次數

surround	enclose	encircle
4304	1502	249

surround（vt.）

❖ 常用句型

> **S + surround + O**

❖ 例句

The CSI officers are still trying to unravel the mystery surrounding the death of the President.
犯罪現場鑑識警官還在嘗試解開環繞總統之死的謎團。

The garden is surrounded by walls.
這花園四周有圍牆環繞。

❖ 常用搭配詞

n. + surrounded by

building, house, square, area, table, valley, pool, nucleus, space, core, spot, mouth, ground, environment, birth, home, girl, stand, clearing, cell, opening, residence, island, stage, town, mountain, head, virus, lawn.

the <u>n.</u> + surrounding N

circumstances, controversy, issues, events, publicity, uncertainty, area, confusion mystery, problems, facts, debate, myths, rumors, secrecy, hype, countryside, space, atmosphere, fears, questions, lake, environment, walls, fields, activity, speculation, darkness, community, scandal, territory, tension, criteria, allegations, woods, hills, taboos, fluid, crowd, sentiment, difficulties, conditions, house, region, factors, drama, intrigue, obscurity, violence.

surrounded by + <u>n.</u>

people, trees, water, controversy, woods, police, walls, flowers, fields, flowers, men, troops, gardens, children, love, farmland, hills, mountains, friends, mirrors, crowds, books, dogs, cards, diamonds, sea, tanks, lawns, supporters, mystery, cameras, strangers.

enclose（vt.）

❖ 常用句型

> **S + enclose + O**

❖ 例句

She lives in a house enclosed by six-foot walls.
她住在一棟周圍有六尺高圍牆的房子。

❖ 常用搭配詞

enclose the + adj. + n.
　square, forest, fields, area.

n. + enclosed by
　area, fields, space.

enclosed by a + n.
　wall, circle, border.

encircle（vt.）

❖ 常用句型

S + encircle + O

❖ 例句

The lake was completely encircled by a road.
這座湖的四周全部被道路環繞。

❖ 常用搭配詞

encircled by a + n.
　band, ring.

encircle the + n.
　globe, town.

綜合整理

surround	四圍環繞在某個人或物，也衍伸表示和某件事情或事件密切相關（如surrounded by controversy充滿爭議），常用在被動語態。
enclose	四圍環繞，尤其是用牆壁或籬笆圍住周圍，目的是和外面區隔分開。主要意義是放在信封中當作附件。
encircle	完全圍繞某個人或物。

Unit 86 偽裝，掩飾

StringNet語料庫出現次數

disguise	camouflage
907	200

disguise（vt.）

❖ 常用句型

S + disguise + O

❖ 例句

She made no attempt to disguise her contempt for her boss.
她毫不掩飾她對她老闆的輕視。
The role of prince was played by a girl, who was disguised as a boy.
王子的角色由一位女孩女扮男裝飾演。

❖ 常用搭配詞

disguise the + _n._
    fact, way, presence, shape, contempt, reality, smile, truth, extent, anxiety, feeling.

disguised as a + _n._
    flower, woman, boy, priest.

camouflage（n.）

❖ 例句

Color change in chameleon has functions in camouflage.
變色龍的色彩變化有隱藏自己的功能。

❖ 常用搭配詞

camouflage + n.

   jacket, square, cream, net, uniform, paint, fatigues, netting, combat,
   dress.

綜合整理

disguise	改變外貌、聲音等以致於別人無法認出真正的身分。也表示掩飾事實或感受。
camouflage	可以當動詞和名詞，因為語料庫中動詞的用法很少，所以在此討論名詞。表示軍人等用樹葉或油漆裝扮成和周遭環境相似以致於不會被發現。另外也指迷彩裝。

Unit 87 彎曲的

StringNet語料庫出現次數

curved	winding	twisted	crooked	bent	tortuous
786	564	456	313	234	142

curved（adj.）

❖ 例句

A buffalo is a beautiful animal with huge, curved horns.
水牛是一種美麗、有巨大彎曲頭角的動物。

❖ 常用搭配詞

curved + n.

　　spaced-time, space, surface, lines, edge, path, walls, spine, bill, arrow, blade, horns, back, shape, nose, knife, sides, ends, roofs, glass, sections, design, handle, cutting, beak, metal, stone, projection, top, pipe, staircase, wings, bone, strip, arms, stairs, iron.

winding（adj.）

❖ 例句

It is dangerous to drive in the mountain because of its winding roads and steep hills.
在這座山開車很危險，因為道路彎曲且坡度很陡。

❖ 常用搭配詞

winding + n.

　road, current, streets, gear, lane, river, path, sheet, staircase, stair, valley, route, house, chain, course, wool, back, track, passage, alleyways, string, corridors, trails, hill, village, channel, drive.

twisted（adj.）

❖ 例句

They found the black box in the twisted wreckage of the plane.
他們在這架飛機扭曲變形的殘骸中找到黑盒子。

❖ 常用搭配詞

twisted + n.

　pair, metal, sheet, rope, tongue, hands, steel, face, wreckage, roots, limbs, trees, trucks, gold, fingers, arms, line, lip, brass, branches.

crooked（adj.）

❖ 例句

His crooked teeth and weird accent made him an obvious classroom victim.
他歪斜的牙齒和古怪的腔調使他在班上常被欺負。

❖ 常用搭配詞

crooked + n.

  teeth, back, nose, stick, leg, finger, figure, lane, street, way, line, elbow, shoulders, face.

bent（adj.）

❖ 例句

He was holding a bent fork.

他手上拿著一個彎曲的叉子。

❖ 常用搭配詞

bent + n.

  head, legs, knees, metal, wire, arms, figure, tower, feather, fork, shoulder, door, line.

tortuous（adj.）

❖ 例句

The kidnappers took a deliberately tortuous route.

綁票的歹徒故意轉彎繞路。

❖ 常用搭配詞

tortuous + n.

  route, journey, path, course, maze.

綜合整理

curved	彎曲有弧度的，通常是天生或刻意做成的（如curved beak有弧度的鳥嘴）。
winding	捲繞蜿蜒的，時常用來形容道路、河流、或繩子。
twisted	多方扭曲變形的（如twisted pair二條互相纏繞的絕緣導線製成的雙絞線），尤其是遭受損壞的結果。
crooked	多方歪斜彎曲變形的，時常用來形容人體部位（如crooked teeth歪斜的牙齒）、河流道路、或掛在牆壁上的圖片歪一邊。另外也指不正派的。
bent	不直的（如bent nail彎曲的指甲）。口語用法也指不正派的。
tortuous	道路或河流迂迴曲折難行的。

Unit 88 網子

StringNet語料庫出現次數

net	web
3128	699

net（n.）

❖ 例句

He never goes camping without bringing a mosquito net.
他去露營一定會帶蚊帳。

❖ 常用搭配詞

n. + net

safety, mosquito, landing, fishing, tax, purse, nerve, adult, drift, sector, camouflage, radio, welfare, tennis, shrimp, nylon, aquarium, breeding, hair, cargo, nest, butterfly, volleyball.

adj. + net

neural, empty, logical, indoor, black, feedforward, local, loose, confiscated, wide, hanging, giant, square, tangled, illegal.

web（n.）

❖ 例句

The books are only available on the Web.
這本書只有在網路上才買得到。

The novel depicts the tangled web of the relationships among the royal family members.
這本小說敘述皇家成員中錯綜複雜的關係。

❖ 常用搭配詞

n. + web

　food, spider, orb, sheet, word.

adj. + web

　complex, tangled, seamless, intricate, complicated, whole, sticky, fine, black, global, vast, broken sinister, wide, interlocking, organizational, radiating.

綜合整理

net	泛指網狀物，如漁網或足球網等球類運動使用的網子。現在常用來指網路（the Net），和the Web相似。
web	表示蜘蛛網，錯綜複雜的事物，現在常用來指網路（the Web = the World Wide Web = www.），和the Net相似。

Unit 89 預期，預料

StringNet語料庫出現次數

expect	anticipate
28039	2337

expect（vt.）

❖ 常用句型

> **S + expect +（somebody/something）to do something**
> **S + expect + that 子句**

❖ 例句

She didn't expect him to help her.
她沒有期望他幫助她。
I didn't expect that there would be so much traffic.
我沒有預料到交通會如此擁擠。

❖ 常用搭配詞

be + adj. + to expect

　reasonable, unrealistic, unreasonable, entitled, realistic, wrong, fair,
　foolish, unfair, natural, logical, unwise, ridiculous, right, sensible,
　inappropriate, rational, naïve, possible, impractical.

adv. + expect

reasonably, normally, hardly, widely, fully, least, confidently, seriously, realistically, originally, obviously, naturally, certainly, initially, previously, legitimately, possibly, currently, naively, presumably, socially.

anticipate（vt.）

❖ 常用句型

S + anticipate + N
S + anticipate doing something
S + anticipate + that 子句

❖ 例句

People stayed home and anticipated the hurricane.
大家都待在家嚴陣以待，準備颶風來臨。
I didn't anticipate having to give a speech.
我沒有預料會需要上台演講。
No one could have anticipated that the typhoon would change its direction.
沒有人能料到這個颱風會轉向。

❖ 常用搭配詞

anticipate the + n. of

kind, possibility, actions, events, consequences, presence, needs, use, publication, conclusions, reaction, coming, loss, success.

adv. + anticipated

eagerly, widely, originally, correctly, readily, previously, seriously.

綜合整理

expect	等待計畫中會發生的事，預料某件事情可能發生。也指期盼某人做某事。
anticipate	預料某件事會發生，並且做好準備。也表示期待某件快樂的事情發生。

Unit 90 遇到

StringNet語料庫出現次數

meet	encounter
32884	2690

meet（vt.）

❖ 常用句型

> **S + meet + O**

❖ 例句

He met her at a birthday party and fell in love with her at first sight.

他在一個生日派對上認識她，對她一見鍾情。

❖ 常用搭配詞

meet + n.

people, representatives, demand, president, john（人名）, friends, member, needs, children, standards, expectations, opposition, men, women, clients, girls, resistance, commitments, strangers, requests.

adv. + meet

already, finally, regularly, usually, rarely, recently, frequently, normally, eventually, probably, previously, subsequently, immediately, consistently, suddenly, occasionally, briefly.

encounter（vt.）

❖ 常用句型

> **S + encounter + O**

❖ 例句

Don't lose heart when encountering difficulties.
遇到困難時不要灰心。

❖ 常用搭配詞

encounter + _n._

difficulties, problems, resistance, opposition, people, prejudice, groups, god, fog, cases, conflict, frustration, movement, men.

adv. + encounter

frequently, commonly, rarely, previously, regularly, normally, suddenly, occasionally, recently, inevitably, repeatedly, probably, directly, invariably, consistently, constantly, eventually, undoubtedly, subsequently.

綜合整理

meet	有多種意義，可以指事先安排的會面、巧遇、或是初次認識。也和encounter同樣表示遭遇困難或問題（如meet opposition遭遇反對）。在語料庫中常用來表示符合或滿足（如meet requirements滿足要求）。
encounter	遇到困難或問題。在正式用法中也表示巧遇。

索引

秀威經典   學語言15　PD0058

英語辭彙不NG
——StringNet教你使用英文同義字（III）

作　　者/李路得
責任編輯/杜國維
圖文排版/賴英珍
封面設計/蔡瑋筠

出版策劃/秀威經典
發 行 人/宋政坤
法律顧問/毛國樑　律師
印製發行/秀威資訊科技股份有限公司
　　　　　114台北市內湖區瑞光路76巷65號1樓
　　　　　電話：+886-2-2796-3638　傳真：+886-2-2796-1377
　　　　　http://www.showwe.com.tw
劃撥帳號/19563868　戶名：秀威資訊科技股份有限公司
　　　　　讀者服務信箱：service@showwe.com.tw
展售門市/國家書店（松江門市）
　　　　　104台北市中山區松江路209號1樓
　　　　　電話：+886-2-2518-0207　傳真：+886-2-2518-0778
網路訂購/秀威網路書店：http://store.showwe.tw
　　　　　國家網路書店：http://www.govbooks.com.tw

2017年12月　BOD一版
定價：600元

國家圖書館出版品預行編目

英語辭彙不NG：StringNet教你使用英文同義字.
(III) / 李路得著. -- 一版. -- 臺北市：秀威經典,
2017.12
　　面；　公分. -- (學語言 ; 15)
BOD版
ISBN 978-986-94998-9-7(平裝)

1. 英語　2. 同義詞　3. 詞彙

805.124   106019054

讀者回函卡

感謝您購買本書，為提升服務品質，請填妥以下資料，將讀者回函卡直接寄回或傳真本公司，收到您的寶貴意見後，我們會收藏記錄及檢討，謝謝！如您需要了解本公司最新出版書目、購書優惠或企劃活動，歡迎您上網查詢或下載相關資料：http:// www.showwe.com.tw

您購買的書名：_____

出生日期：_____年_____月_____日

學歷：□高中 (含) 以下　　□大專　　□研究所 (含) 以上

職業：□製造業　□金融業　□資訊業　□軍警　□傳播業　□自由業
　　　□服務業　□公務員　□教職　　□學生　□家管　□其它____

購書地點：□網路書店　□實體書店　□書展　□郵購　□贈閱　□其他

您從何得知本書的消息？

　□網路書店　□實體書店　□網路搜尋　□電子報　□書訊　□雜誌

　□傳播媒體　□親友推薦　□網站推薦　□部落格　□其他_____

您對本書的評價：(請填代號　1.非常滿意　2.滿意　3.尚可　4.再改進)

　封面設計____　版面編排____　內容____　文／譯筆____　價格____

讀完書後您覺得：

　□很有收穫　□有收穫　□收穫不多　□沒收穫

對我們的建議：_____

_____

_____

_____

11466
台北市內湖區瑞光路 76 巷 65 號 1 樓

秀威資訊科技股份有限公司 　　　　收

BOD 數位出版事業部

⋯⋯⋯⋯⋯⋯⋯⋯⋯⋯⋯⋯⋯⋯⋯⋯⋯⋯⋯⋯⋯⋯⋯

（請沿線對折寄回，謝謝！）

姓　　名：＿＿＿＿＿＿＿＿＿　年齡：＿＿＿＿＿　性別：□女　□男

郵遞區號：□□□□□

地　　址：＿＿＿＿＿＿＿＿＿＿＿＿＿＿＿＿＿＿＿＿＿＿＿＿

聯絡電話：(日) ＿＿＿＿＿＿＿＿＿＿＿　(夜) ＿＿＿＿＿＿＿＿＿＿

E-mail：＿＿＿＿＿＿＿＿＿＿＿＿＿＿＿＿＿＿＿＿＿＿＿＿